MASON
&
JULIA

WILLOW WINTERS
WALL STREET JOURNAL & USA TODAY BESTSELLING AUTHOR

"Love is more than words; my heart can tell you that." - DLS

To Donna, always an inspiration.

From USA Today best-selling author Willow Winters comes an intense romance with second chances, secrets and a twist.

Mason Thatcher gave me chills when I first laid eyes on him. The good kind. The kind that make your body ache, and your heart hammer.

It's not fair that his touch eased my pain. That his lips on mine made my worries vanish. That his love gave me a reason to breathe again.

With him I felt complete, as if fate had given me a second chance.

Then I learned the truth: the sins and secrets of what had really brought us together. I only hope we could go back. I never could have imagined this.

You Are My Reason is book 1 in the You Are Mine duet and should be read first.

You Are My Reason

CHAPTER 1

MASON

"**Y**ou should be thanking me for cleaning up your mess," my father says snidely from where he's seated in his high-back desk chair. His fingers grip the leather arms and his thumbs rub gently back and forth across the brass studs.

Though the blinds are closed, the tall windows behind my father fill the large office with fading light from the evening sunset.

Looking over my shoulder, I narrow my gaze at him, still holding a random law textbook I've taken from the floor-to-ceiling shelves that line the walls of his office. The room smells like old books. With the dark wood, tan leather and deep red Beaumont rug, the decor reeks of old money and that's exactly what this room represents.

That and bullshit.

Lies and corruption are what have kept this room in its current state for generations. I've pretended for so long that it wasn't true. But now that I've learned what my father's done to get this "esteemed" position ... I can't turn a blind eye to it anymore. His actions are undeniable and unforgivable.

I huff a small laugh, not letting him see how affected I am. "For the last time," I say as I shut the book and smirk at him, "it wasn't my mess."

I'm not admitting to a damn thing. Not even to my own father. In this city, one slipup could send you tumbling into an early grave like my mother. I'm not responsible for the mess my father's referring to and I refuse to take the blame.

I don't trust him. I don't trust anyone any longer.

My father's face reddens before he picks up a cup of hot coffee. He holds the black mug with both hands, blowing across the top and refusing to back down.

"You would have gone through hell—"

"No, I wouldn't have," I say, cutting him off, although my voice doesn't reflect any emotion whatsoever. This is a turning point in our relationship. Instead of his disappointment creeping under my skin, it's the other way around. I look him in the eye as I add, "I would have been just fine."

A moment passes where the only sound is the ticking of the large clock on the right side of the room. "It wasn't my mess you cleaned up, and we both know it." He's the first to look away but instead of showing remorse, his expression only reflects his anger.

"Did you need anything else?" I ask. I just want to get the hell out of here and back to the construction site. This office reminds me of my grandfather, a man I loved and trusted. But he was a man who turned out to be just like all the other powerful men in this city. Ruled by corruption, driven by greed, imperfect. *Devastated* is the word a former therapist would use to describe my reaction when I found out the truth about my family.

"I'm tired of you getting into trouble," my father says and I scoff. This is the first time in my life I've truly been in control of myself. No more fucking around, starting trouble. These recent events have been sobering. When I was a hormone-filled teenager dealing with grief and anger, it was easy to act out and pick fights. Caused first by the death of my grandfather and then later, my mother.

At thirty-three and on my own, I'm not like that anymore. I finally have my life together ... all but the ties to my father. It's a tangled mess of lies and offshore bank accounts. Much like the dealings of the elite who rule this city.

The thought makes my gaze fall to the floor before I look back up to the shelves and mindlessly scan the spines of the antique texts.

Being aware of what my father did makes all those old

memories of losing my mother surface. My stomach churns and my blood heats, the adrenaline coursing in my veins pushing me to confront the man I no longer know.

I bring a clenched fist to my mouth as I clear my throat and take a few steps toward him. He's the one who called this meeting, demanded it really. But he hasn't even risen from his chair. Lazy prick.

"I don't know what you're talking about," I answer him easily. "I haven't got a single problem on my mind." I give him a polite smile and keep a charming look on my face. It only makes him angrier and I love every second of his pissed-off expression. He thought I'd feel as if I owed him.

I don't owe him a damn thing.

I may be just like him in looks. Tall, dark and handsome, or so I've been told. I've perfected a brilliant smile with an air of ease that's made to fool and seduce the world at large. It makes sense that he's a lawyer. It's the family business but if it wasn't, it'd still be the profession most apt for my father.

"You need to quit this charade and do what you're told, Mason." He stands from his seat quickly, his chair rolling backward until it hits the wall. It disturbs the blinds and streams of dim light flicker into the room.

"I don't need to do anything but breathe and pay taxes."

He could order me around like that all he wanted back when I was a child or before I knew the truth, but now I have no respect for the man in front of me. I'm disgusted by him and caught on the edge of what's right and wrong. I should turn him in to the authorities and let him rot. I grit my teeth as I stare back at him. It's what's right, but I can't bring myself to send my own father to prison.

A low hum of admonishment deep in his throat makes the smirk on my face widen into a smile.

"I have my own company, my own life—" I start but my father cuts me off. Nothing new there.

"You were born a Thatcher, and you'll die a Thatcher." The words leave a chill across my skin. That's the crux of the problem. I was born into this life and I can't run from it. Plus my company is in debt to him. It was a rookie mistake I made back before I knew what I was doing. When I didn't see him for the man he really is.

"Why do you even care what I do?" I finally ask him. His precious reputation is just fine now that I'm an adult and I've moved on from the fuckup I used to be. "I'm not the one coming to you—"

"*She* did," he answers simply with a spark in his eyes and the corners of his lips upturned as if that's all the ammunition he needs. In some respects, he's right. All the people in this city know where I come from and what it means to be a Thatcher. They know I have money and power behind me. That's all anyone here cares about anyway. New York is all about the bottom dollar.

Nonchalantly shrugging my shoulders, I stride closer to

the desk, bracing myself by gripping the back of the chair opposite him. "You decided how to deal with her without vetting what she said." I meet his glare easily, willing him to tell me again how he *saved* me. "She didn't have anything on me. She couldn't have done anything." My voice rises toward the end of my statement and I hate that I've shown him this weak side of me. Even if only for a moment.

Control. I thrive with control.

A heavy breath leaves him as he stares back with pure hate but he doesn't say a word. I knew he wouldn't. He's wrong. Dead wrong and ruined if I open my mouth to anyone. He took the initiative so I'd owe him, but in reality we both know that he owes me now.

"It's your fuckup, not mine." I practically spit out the words and shove the chair forward as I turn to leave him. My body's tense and the anger continues to rise. I try not to let it show. I hate that I can't control myself around this prick. Everyone else I can handle, but my own father, not so much.

"Mason!" he calls after me. His voice turns to white noise as the blood rushing in my ears gets louder and louder, drowning out all the bullshit.

The second I open his office door, he goes silent. He'll never let anyone hear us fighting. *Never.* Secrets are always kept behind closed doors. It's a family rule.

The door shuts with a loud *thunk* and as I walk down the empty hall, the thin carpeting muffles the sound of my black leather oxfords smacking against the ground at an incessant pace.

Miss Geist looks up from her spot at her desk. The wrinkles around her eyes deepen as she tilts her head and gives me that familiar smile she always has for me. It's one that says: *Oh, what have you done now?*

Through the years, even after my mother's death, Miss Theresa Geist has given me that look. She's the only one who showed me any genuine regret and kindness when I had to deal with my mother's passing. She's a good person. I have no idea what she's doing here working for a man like my father.

She clutches the small pendant on her thin silver necklace and her forbearing smile changes to something more reserved when I look back at her. It's instantaneous and makes me halt in my steps. I know I must look pissed; I'm beyond furious. It's been two days since my father told me what he'd done all those months ago and my anger hasn't waned one bit. Deep down I think I knew what he'd done back then, even if he never admitted it until now. I wish he hadn't. The whole situation makes me sick.

"He's being a dick," I mutter, waiting for the old lady to be a little more at ease. She doesn't know a thing that goes on outside of the office and I don't owe her an explanation, but I can't help myself.

"Now, now," she says with a bit of playfulness although I can tell she's still shaken. She's not used to seeing me like this.

Not in the last decade, at least.

I give her a gentle smile and wink, putting on the act I use so well. Maybe I have a soft spot for her.

"Have a good night, Mr. Thatcher," she tells me as she shuffles the papers on her desk, seeming somewhat less disturbed.

It's enough that it settles me and I push open the double doors leading to the entrance with both hands and keep moving. The sound of my shoes pacing on the granite and the open air of the lobby filled with chatter soothe me.

But only for a moment.

It's not until I leave the building that my true feelings surface. The mask fades, and fear sets in. I didn't know what my father was capable of.

I had an inkling, but I thought I'd always imagined it. I'd thought my memories weren't quite right. It's not that I expected more from him; I just hate that I was right.

What's done is done and I can't stop what's been set in motion.

Chapter 2

Julia

Bloodred lips. The silver tube in my hand is labeled Black Honey, my favorite color. I've worn it since my freshman year of college and although I've experimented with other colors at times, it's always been a staple in my beauty bag. Pressing my lips together, I smack them once as I examine myself in the mirror.

My complexion is flawless thanks to the full-coverage foundation I'm wearing. My lashes are thick and long, and I've got just a hint of blush. It's a timeless look, classic and clean. And it hides everything. My reddened skin and the dark circles under my eyes are nowhere to be found.

I don't look like the person I've become. This woman in

the reflection, she's who I used to be. A very large part of me wants *this* woman back. I want to smile like I used to and hear the sound of a genuine laugh from my own lips.

My heart pangs and stops that thought in its place.

He'll never laugh again. It's as if any small moment of time that passes where he's forgotten for even a second is a disgrace. My eyes fall and I slip the cap back on the tube of lipstick, tossing it into the pouch on my vanity.

No matter what I do, every little thing reminds me of him.

Trivial things, like the color of the granite he insisted we purchase when we remodeled this place together. The knobs on the bathroom drawers he hated and never failed to complain about. The change he left in the cup holder in the Bentley. The pile of dimes and pennies that clink together when I drive over speed bumps or a pothole. The same small coins I refuse to touch. He put them there, and I can't bring myself to move them.

Freaking pieces of metal render me useless.

It may seem pathetic, but not to me. From my perspective, I'm being as strong as I can. I face the New York City judgment every day, putting on a brave face and going about my life, my new normal.

All the while I shove everything I'm feeling deep down inside. *That's healthy, right?*

I won't let them see me crumble. There are those who want to. I could practically hear them licking their lips months ago when my world fell apart.

Julia Summers, born into wealth and raised on the Upper East Side. She always did everything by the book and married young to her high school sweetheart, Jace Anderson. With a loving family, a handsome and doting husband and the social life every young woman in Manhattan dreams of, Jules had a picture-perfect life. Until her husband suddenly passed away at the age of twenty-eight, leaving the twenty-seven-year-old woman widowed and alone for the first time in her life.

Twenty-eight now and numerous months since the tragic accident.

They're waiting to see what I'll do next. Pens to the papers and cameras ready. There's nothing better for the gossipmongers. It's to be expected. Being in Page Six is how I've made my life.

They'd love to see me fall and I have, but not in front of their eyes. I'll keep my hair pinned up and my concealer on thick.

I know what they say, though. This town whispers, especially in the circles I run in. They don't need to see the truth to figure it out themselves. There are rumors of leaning too heavily on alcohol for comfort. I don't command enough loyalty for discretion; every member of my household staff has sold out to the tabloids looking for a hint of what goes on behind these walls. Living on the Upper East Side, every single person who struts in front of my home is looking for a crack in my veneer.

What's ironic is that there's no glamour here, nothing noteworthy. Just a woman who cries herself to sleep at least once a week still. A woman who's struggling to move on because she's never been with anyone else. I suppose it's what I get, though. I loved posing for the cameras and practically lived for regular mentions in the gossip columns. This is what I deserve. They wanted in my life and I let them. I can't expect them to be shut out now.

Days have turned to weeks and weeks to months. Now that my husband's been gone for nearly eight months, I have plenty of cracks in this so-called perfect life. I'm still shattered but I'm working on gluing little pieces back into place.

I glance at myself as I tug down my dress just slightly and smooth out the black lace. *It's time to face the music.*

I clear my throat as I turn off the light and grab my phone, checking the text again.

Are you sure you don't need me to pick you up?

Kat's a sweetheart. She's always looking out for me. Of all my friends, she's the one who still texts me religiously, which is insane because she's constantly working and I have no idea how she finds the time.

My fingers *tap, tap, tap* away an answer. *I've got it. Leaving now.*

The Penrose is only twenty minutes away if there's no traffic. Seeing how it's 9:00 p.m. on a Friday night, I'm prepared to sit in the back of a taxi for half the night.

A light sigh slips past my lips as I bend down to pick up my favorite Louboutins. With a row of spikes up the back and red-lacquered soles, they have exactly the touch of color and attitude I would've worn back then. I almost second-guess the simple black dress I've picked out. It's a nod to Audrey Hepburn. But looking over my shoulder at the darkened bathroom mirror, all I see is one of the options I had for Jace's funeral.

I would've worn this dress last year before it all happened. Back when I was happy and everything was how it was supposed to be. And don't I want to be that girl again? I want to find a way to move forward on a new path.

Holding the heels in one hand and the iron banister in the other, I descend the winding staircase.

I'm not that woman any longer; I've changed. I accept that, but I don't love who I am now. The crying and feeling sorry for myself. I need something. A change and some light in all the darkness. Eight months of a pity party and being stuck in a rut is long enough. I'd like to say that Jace wouldn't want to see me like this, but I don't even know what Jace would want for me. I've quit wearing my wedding ring, although it still sits on my nightstand. I'm ready to find out who I am without him beside me.

Before I open the front door, I glimpse out the large stained glass window in the foyer. It's nothing but gray outside, and the hustle and bustle is only a fraction of what it could be.

Heavy rain greets me when I step onto my small porch. I decided not to bother with an umbrella, simply grabbing a stylish trench coat on my way outside. Quickly taking the steps to the street out front, I hail a cab. My heels click as I wrap the belt around me and tie my coat tight when the first taxi comes to a slow stop in front of me.

I could have called for someone to do this, to order me a cab so it would be waiting. I could ask for help with so many things. I'd rather do it myself, though.

The light breeze and rain feel real. The rain is cold to the touch and I'm sure I'll be regretting my decision soon. But it's something different. I don't want anyone's help. I just need time.

Climbing into the taxi, I shake off the gathered rain from my jacket; the inside of the cab is warm and welcoming. I push the hair out of my face and say, "Penrose, please."

"You got it," the cabby says as he glances over his shoulder to look at me. His thinning black hair is oiled over and he's more than a little overweight. The buttons on his striped shirt are straining to keep it shut.

I can see curiosity in his eyes but just as he opens his mouth to ask something, I don't know what, I turn to look out the closed window and thank him.

Everything outside is wet and dreary. The people walking by move quickly and a couple only about ten feet away are fighting over an umbrella. It's a cute little struggle though and the tall man in a navy blue Henley lets the woman win. She's dressed in formal work clothes, while he's in casual attire. But as soon as she takes full control of the umbrella, she walks closer to him and he wraps his arm around her waist.

I rip my eyes away and pick at my nails. It's little things like what I just witnessed that I find unbearable. I bite the inside of my cheek and hold back the bitterness.

Luckily, the driver gets the picture. I'm not in the mood to talk and the cab moves ahead, taking me away from my sanctuary and toward another test.

That's what these things really are. Tests.

It's only in this moment that I realize I'm really doing it. I've put it off so many times over the last eight months. I've given so many excuses for not meeting up with the girls.

Why today? I don't know. My heart sinks thinking that maybe I'm really getting over my husband's death.

As much as I want to be the woman I once was, happy and carefree, I don't want to forget him.

I lay my head back on the headrest and close my eyes, my clutch in my lap. Jace gave it to me last Christmas. I snort at the thought, running my fingers over the smooth, hot pink leather. More like I picked it out and he paid for it.

I close my eyes and take in a deep breath. It's calming riding in a quiet cab at night in the city. The quiet rumble of the engine and the white noise of the rain are a serene mix.

The last day I saw my husband was when we were watching my nephew Everett, so my sister could have a mother-daughter day with Lexi. It's rare I see my family at all; everyone is so busy with their own lives and my sister is much older than I am... so we're not exactly close. I still love them though.

The thought of my nephew brings a smile to my face. With sandy blond hair that just barely covers his big blue eyes and a wide smile, you can't help but smile back at him. He was only a few months old back then. A brand-new life in this world. That's the way it works, isn't it? Life and death go hand in hand.

I glance forward out the windshield and give a slight start when we stop far away from Second Avenue where the bar is located; a bit of traffic is holding us up.

The cabby notices my reaction in the rearview mirror and shrugs as he says, "We should be out of it soon." He's tense at the wheel, probably expecting me to snap at him, maybe blame him for taking this particular route. More guilt washes over me. I hate spreading negativity simply by being so ... gloom and doom with the air surrounding me. I'm not an ice queen, or at least I don't mean to be.

I give him a soft smile, placing my clutch in the middle seat. "I figured we'd run into something," I say easily. My voice comes out even and calm. It's the voice I use with my mother. The kind of tone that says: *I'm okay, just tired.*

The cabby shifts, making the leather seat grumble and he tries to make small chat.

I nod my head and answer politely, but keep everything short and to the point. I can be accommodating with others and I truly want to do so. I'm tired of being alone and pushing others away. It's just harder than I thought it would be after how I've been since Jace passed.

After a moment of quiet, I look out the window again. The rain's nearly stopped, and the sidewalks are instantly crowded as a result. The people were always there, waiting under awnings for protection. Not many people like to venture into weather that washes away your makeup and ruins even the best put-together look.

They were waiting and ready to keep moving just the same. All they needed was a small break before setting out again. The only question is if there will be another awning to save them when the brutal downpour comes back.

The cabby stops and my eyes whip up to the sign on my right, my heart beating faster as I watch dozens of people walking in front of me on the sidewalk. Each going wherever it is that life has taken them. I don't know if I'm ready, but at least I'm here.

"Miss?" the cabby asks after I remain where I am in this cozy seat. I shake my head slightly with quick motions and play off my hesitation, paying him and leaving a big tip as well. He deserves it for having to suffer my company.

"Have a good night," I tell him as I slip out, my heels hitting the slick asphalt and the door shutting behind me with a resounding click.

CHAPTER 3

MASON

It figures it would stop pouring the second I get in here. The bar is packed and the cacophony of guests chatting and glasses clinking welcome me. I can get lost in the crowds. I know the people here see me, but they don't know me.

This bar in particular is one of my favorites. It's always full. Its tufted leather seats are constantly filled, and the warm rich tones of the wooden ceiling and brick walls make it feel like home somehow.

My suit is nothing fancy, nothing that will stand out in here. Which is how I want it. I run my fingers through my hair and shake away the rain as I shrug off my jacket and toss it over the barstool at the very end.

It's been a long day and the last thing I need is to go home alone. As soon as my eyes lift, the bartender is on me. I think her name is Patricia. She's in here every weekend.

"Whiskey?" she asks me. She never stops moving, shoveling ice into short glasses and pouring liquor like a pro. Unlike the other women in here, she's not looking for a man with deep pockets. She doesn't do chitchat either, which is another reason I like sitting in this section. The biggest reason is that it's out of the way, somewhere I can simply blend in and watch.

"Double," I answer her with a nod and slip my cell phone out from my jacket pocket. I've only been gone from the office for two hours, but I've got a dozen emails waiting for my attention. A huff of a grunt leaves me as a text from Liam pops up.

You coming out tonight?

Already out, I answer him as the glass hits the polished bar top and Patricia slides it over to me.

My phone pings as I lift the tumbler to my lips and let the cool liquor burn all the way down, warming my chest.

Where at?

I contemplate telling him. I like Liam. A lot. If I had any friends, he'd be one of them. But and after talking to my father today, I don't want to be around a damn soul.

A sarcastic laugh makes me grin as I realize I've come to a crowded bar to be alone. It's the truth, though. You're always surrounded by people in this city; there's never a place to hide unless it's in plain sight.

I down the rest of my drink and tap the heavy glass against the bar top as I consider what to tell him. That's when I hear it. Almost as if daring me to stay alone any longer, it's the gentle sound of a feminine laugh. It's genuine and it rings out clear in the bar even though it's soft.

It's a soothing sound, a calming force in the chaos that surrounds us. Everything around me fades except for the woman who uttered that sweet sound.

The smooth glass stays still as I look down the bar in search of her.

The rest of the crowd doesn't seem to notice as they continue with whatever the hell they're saying and doing, but my eyes are drawn to my left. Through the throng of people, I just barely get a glimpse of her.

Dark brunette hair that's pulled back; pale skin covered in black lace.

A man at the opposite end leans away from the bar, digging in his back pocket for his wallet and giving me a clear view of her.

Those dark red lips attract my gaze first. She licks her bottom lip before picking up a large glass of deep red wine. The color matches her lips perfectly. She smiles at something and her shoulders shake as she laughs, making the dark liquid swirl in her glass and bringing a blush to her high cheekbones.

She tosses her hair to the side and her fingers tease the

ends as she brings her tendrils over one shoulder, wrapping them around her finger while she sips her wine.

It's when she looks away from whomever she's been giving her attention to that my curiosity is piqued.

Without their eyes on her, her expression morphs into something else. I finally see her eyes, the lightest of blues, and that's when I really see her. Not just the image of what she's portraying.

Pain is clear as day.

It's the lie though, how fucking good she was at hiding it, that's what really gets me. Even I was fooled.

People can hide behind a smile or a laugh; every soul in here can pretend to be someone and something they're not.

The truth is always there though and I'm damn good at recognizing it. Your eyes can never hide two things: age and emotion. Hers speak to me in a way nothing else can.

But had I never looked just then when she thought no one was watching, she never would have shown me willingly.

She straightens her back and I see her profile, her expression. The corners of my lips turn down. Not only do I know her pain, I know her name. I know everything about her.

Julia Summers.

My blood chills as she turns back to the table, the smile on her face slipping back into position just as the man at the end of the bar steps forward, obscuring her from my vision. As if the moment of clarity and recognition was just for me in that moment. Like fate wanted me to know how close I was to her.

I keep my eyes on the bar, doing my best to listen, but her voice is silent or lost in the mix of chatter throughout the crowded place.

"Another?" Patricia's voice sounds close, closer than she usually is. I lift my head to see her standing right in front of me, both hands on the bar and waiting.

I nod my head with my brows pinched, shaking off the mix of emotions. This city is a small place with worlds always colliding, but I've never seen her in person. Only in a photograph. Only that once. I'm sure it's her, though.

The ice clinks in the glass and I watch as the liquid slips over each cube, cracking them and filling the crevices.

"You okay?" Patricia asks me. It's odd. In the year or so since I've been coming here, she's never bothered to make small talk. It's why I don't mind her.

I give her a tight smile as I reply, "I'm fine." I reach her eyes and widen my smile, relaxing my posture as I lean back slightly.

She eyes me warily as she mutters, "You don't look fine."

It takes me a moment before I shrug it off and say, "I'm all right, just tired."

She nods once and goes back to minding her own business, sliding me the whiskey and moving on to other customers.

I tap my pointer finger against the glass, looking casually down the bar.

She's hidden from view, but I know she's there.

CHAPTER 4

JULIA

My body tingles with another sip of cabernet.

It's my third glass and it's only tasting sweeter on my lips. The tips of my fingers always feel the turning point first when I drink. That familiar buzz that makes my body feel a bit heavy and my mind light.

"I can't believe your license plate says *Alimony*," Maddie says into her wineglass as she snickers again. She's laughing so hard that the white zinfandel splashes onto her lips, but she doesn't care. She merely smiles and takes a large gulp.

Suzette answers with a shrug and a cocky smirk, "The asshole had it coming to him." Her bright pink lipstick smudges against her glass of Long Island iced tea and she wipes it away with her napkin as Maddie continues to laugh. Sue's given herself a makeover since her divorce is now finalized. Currently she's sporting jet-black hair cut into a blunt bob and bangs to go with her snippy attitude.

"Please tell me he saw it when you left the courthouse today. Please?" Maddie practically begs, still grinning from ear to ear.

Maddie's young and naive and thinks Prince Charming is somewhere out there, so you should always be ready. Sue has a marriage, a divorce, and fifteen years on Maddie, so between the three of us, we have as many opinions on love as we do rounds of drinks.

Sue's plastered-on smile slips and she tries to hide it with a shrug as she takes another sip. Her license plate is just one more way for Sue to make fun of her divorce before anyone else can. Her ex put her through hell and she came out cold as ice to all men. Well, except the ones she likes to sink her claws into after a few Long Islands.

Sue leans back in the white leather booth, keeping the glass in her hand and shrugs again as she says, "What says 'fuck you, motherfucker' better than taking his red Ferrari in the proceedings and getting *that* license plate?"

Kat pipes up from her spot in the booth, rolling her eyes and taking a sip of her Pepsi before she says, "I think it says, 'don't touch this bitch' to every man in the city."

A sly smile slips onto Sue's face. "Thank goodness ... that's exactly what I was going for," she says, setting her drink down then stretching her arms over her head. "Maybe all these bastards will finally leave me alone then." The other girls start to howl at that and I join in, although my heart's not in it. My nerves are shot just being out here tonight. Sue's directly across from me and both of us are seated at the ends of the semicircular booth. Kat's to my right, then Maddie.

"Another round?" The waiter startles me and I nearly spill my glass as I gasp and back away. All the poor guy did was offer me another drink and I practically had a heart attack. Several distant gazes turn in our direction as my own table watches me like there's something wrong with me and I do what I do best, I play it off and let out a small laugh. Maybe I'm even more like Sue than I realized.

"Sorry," I say a bit too loud. Exaggerating how tipsy I am, I gently place my hand on the waiter's arm. His starched white shirt feels crisp under my fingers as I lean in and sweetly say, "I'm so sorry, I hope I didn't spill any on you."

That's all it takes for everyone to go about their own business, but my heart's still beating wildly. A few stares linger. I'm aware the people in here recognize me; they probably think I shouldn't be out or that I'm "having a moment." Looking across the room, I'm frozen by a pair of eyes I know all too well.

They belong to a woman in her late sixties, Margo Pierce. She's an heiress and an influential investor in the city. Her large sapphire cocktail rings appear even more over the top as she holds a simple glass of champagne with both hands. For a woman in her sixties, she wears her age well. From her perky breasts to the delicate skin around her eyes, not an inch of her hasn't been through some procedure or another. All the work she's had is very tastefully done, though.

The last time I saw her was at a casino up north, the night I got the phone call. I can still remember the dings and bells of the slot machines and the bright, colorful lights. Still remember the weight of the glass of rosé in my right hand as I sat perched on a barstool in the center of the casino. At the Mohegan Sun, the bar is elevated. I could see nearly a hundred of the other guests playing slots and sitting at the card tables; it was packed that night.

Just like tonight, I was with the girls and we were enjoying ourselves and the atmosphere. We were taking a break from roulette to grab cocktails and Sue was cursing out her soon-to-be ex-husband for prolonging their divorce when my phone rang. I only picked it up because it was odd for my mother to call me so late.

Kat leaned in to order from the bartender as I placed the phone to my ear, turning a bit to my left for a hint of privacy. As much as I could get in such a crowded place, anyway. I didn't show them that anything was unusual, keeping a pleasant smile on my face as I answered.

When I heard my mother's voice on the other end, the

smile vanished and the vibrant night life, chatter, and sounds from the machines turned to dead air.

I could barely make out my mother's voice, just a few words here and there, but I knew something was wrong. Very wrong. I needed to hear better, so I stood and started walking. I didn't know where I was going, all I knew was that I needed to find a less noisy location.

My heart raced, and the shock caused my body temperature to drop so low that I was shivering.

He's dead. I heard her words clear as day as I got to the front of the casino. My heels clipped the large rug at the entrance. I stumbled forward, my short dress riding up and one heel nearly falling off. My knees hit the hard granite flooring and the phone fell from my hand.

Jace is dead. That's what she said.

I imagine the people around me at the time thought I was drunk. I would have assumed that if I'd seen someone fall the way I had.

Margo Pierce was there to help me. Those damn cocktail rings were digging painfully into my arm as she helped lift me up. I stood there on wobbly legs just trying to breathe, but when I looked into her eyes, I could tell she knew.

I knew in that moment it was real. I could lie to myself, or I could have hung up and driven home, all the while in denial. But the sympathy in her eyes was damning.

I rip my eyes away from hers at the other side of the bar

and return back to the girls, back to tonight, leaving that night in the past right where it belongs. I ignore the way my hand itches to drain the wine and order another cabernet and then another while I push my hair back over my shoulders, trying to relax. Trying to shake off the unwanted memory.

"I think you're flagged," Kat says into her glass even as her eyes meet mine. Her sandy brunette hair is colored with a subtle ombre and she's applied her eyeliner in a cat-eye fashion. I don't know why, but I can't stop looking at it. Like if I can just concentrate on her makeup, everything else will leave me alone.

"No such thing," Sue says, quick to come to my defense, an asymmetric grin gracing her lips. "Drink up, girly." She gives me a wink and it forces a smile to my face. It didn't take long for the girls to come find me that night, crying alone in the back of our limo.

With a burn pricking at the back of my eyes, I blink a few times to keep the tears at bay. It was months and months ago, but sometimes the pain comes back full force. I don't know that it will ever go away and if it does, surely that would be a tragedy. I don't know where grief and mourning end and my life begins again, but I'd like to find it.

Pushing away the nearly empty glass, I watch the dark liquid pool in the bottom and sigh deeply. I can't seem to keep a smile on my face. The once easy mask isn't slipping into place. Progress is all I need, though. I remind myself of my motto: Aim for progress, not perfection.

"Let's talk about something and someone else," I suggest. "Is anyone getting laid? One of us must be getting laid, right? At least Kat?" I arch a brow in her direction but her forehead creases in response and the action is followed by a huff and, "Yeah right." *Shit.* I forgot she and her husband are going through something.

Way to put my foot in my mouth.

My skin pricks at the back of my neck as I feel another set of eyes on me. The anxiousness comes back and I put on my best fake smile, staring straight ahead as Maddie starts listing off what was wrong with her last rendezvous. This one was some guy she met online.

The nagging feeling doesn't quit. I don't know who it is, but someone's watching me. It could be the paparazzi but typically every time I go out, they approach me before I even notice them. I'm a socialite, after all, and I know the intrusion is part of this life.

Debating on taking a casual look over my shoulder, I shake off the paranoia. *It's all in your head*, I tell myself. I thought I felt someone watching me earlier, but maybe I was wrong.

"You know enough time has passed." Sue's comment from across the table gets my attention. I look up to find her dark eyes twinkling with mischievousness.

"Enough time for what?" Maddie questions Sue. Maddie's the quintessential younger sister of our group and I swear most of Sue's comments go right over her head.

Sue motions toward me and it's only then that I take in her words. I clear my throat and look away, feeling a blush rise to my cheeks. "When I said someone else ..." I say playfully and pick up the glass, lifting it high in the air and tilting my head back to get the last few drops.

The girls laugh it off, but there's a certain gravitas in Sue's eyes.

She lowers her voice and looks me in the eye as she says, "We just want you to be happy."

"It's 'we' now?" I ask her, suddenly feeling defensive. They've been talking about me behind my back?

Sue shrugs and Kat's quick to put a hand on top of mine. She twists in her spot and the white leather squeaks under her skinny ass. "We were just making conversation earlier." My brow rises as she takes in a breath and tries to find the right words.

"We want you happy again," Maddie says from her seat next to Kat. Her hands make two sharp motions emphasizing *happy again* as she leans back and looks straight ahead, avoiding my eyes on her.

Oh my God ... is this some kind of intervention? I imagine my face reflects exactly what I'm thinking. Judging by the guilty expressions Kat and Maddie are wearing on their faces, I'm sure it does. Sue is shameless though, back to nursing her drink.

Of course they'd talk about me. I can't explain why it feels like a betrayal, though. Why my throat seems to go dry and itch as if I'm going to cry. Why wouldn't they? Everyone else is.

"Hey, Jules." Kat's voice is soft, placating even.

I pull my hand away from her and suck in a breath. "It's fine," I whisper, grabbing my clutch.

Sue's quick to sit forward and say, "Don't go. It wasn't—"

"Just headed to the powder room," I blurt out. "I just need to freshen up," I tell them with a tight smile, standing up and tugging down my dress.

"Do you want company?" Kat asks, already sliding out behind me.

"I just need a minute," I say and shake my head, giving her pleading eyes. I love them. They only want what's best for me. But don't they know how hard this is? How much it took just to come out here.

I can handle this. I just need something although I'm not sure what that something is. A breath of fresh air, maybe. Or a drink of water or something stronger. I don't know what, but I know I need at least a minute to myself to figure it out.

Chapter 5

Mason

The anxious feeling deep in my gut won't quit. It only gets more intense as Julia walks behind me, politely maneuvering her small frame amid the crowd of people. Watching her from my periphery, I listen to the rhythmic sound of her heels and watch how her hips sway gently.

She doesn't notice me, which is by design, but still it aggravates me. She passes so close behind me on her way to the restrooms that I catch a hint of her sweet scent. No doubt it's perfume, a gentle floral mixed with citrus of some sort but as it fills my lungs, I can't help but grip the bar top tighter to keep myself from following her.

Ever since I caught a glimpse of her, I haven't been able

to move or get her out of my head. For months, I haven't thought twice about her. Each time her picture swept into my head, I pushed it away.

But she's here now, so close that I could touch her.

I can't approach her, though. How fucked up would that be?

I can't cross that line. She doesn't know a damn bit of the truth.

I down the remainder of my whiskey and slide the empty glass forward, pissed off and frustrated.

As I stand abruptly, the stool slides backward and bumps into someone. I turn to look over my shoulder while reaching into my back pocket for my wallet. "Sorry," I say without thinking only to find myself staring directly at Julia.

Her eyes still aren't on me as she waves off my apology, looking at the bottles lining the back of the bar before finally resting her gorgeous blue eyes on me. This close to her I can see they're pale blue with flecks of silver speckled throughout. They're beautiful.

She shakes her head just slightly, making her hair fall off her shoulder and exposing more of her bare skin. "It's fine." Her voice is soft as she walks forward without missing a beat, stepping up to the bar on my right, coming closer. Like a lamb heading into the lion's den, teasing and taunting unknowingly.

She's so close to me, so damn alluring. The black lacy dress clings to her curves. Her hips are seductive and I can just imagine how they'd feel to hold as I took her from behind. I can feel the bartender's eyes flicker to me questioningly as Julia orders, but I can't take my gaze off Julia.

I swallow thickly, leaning my forearms against the bar and attempting to act casual, getting that much closer to her.

She doesn't know anything about how we're linked and she doesn't have to. She'll never know the truth and this is my chance to learn more about who the pretty face in the picture is.

"Julia, right?" My heart pounds, questioning why the hell would I admit that I know anything at all about her. I don't intend to lie to her, though. Nothing but lies of omission. I've heard her name in social circles. Her family is well known so I doubt she'll be surprised that I recognize her.

"Jules," she corrects me warmly, now looking at me differently than she did a moment ago. She seems to do a double take and a hint of playfulness sparkles in her eyes. It's as if I'm suddenly what she's been looking for. Or maybe *who* she's been waiting for.

"Ah, Jules." I tap my fingers on the bar and glance away for a moment. *What the fuck am I doing?* This isn't just playing with fire, this is worse. It's asking to be burned and shoving my fists into the coals.

Patricia sets two shots of what look like chilled tequila in front of Jules. I watch with interest as she throws the first one back without thinking twice. Her slender fingers slip around the second one, ready to down it as well.

The pain comes off her in waves. She's drowning it in alcohol. She's good at hiding her emotions on the surface, but her actions speak so much louder than words.

"For a moment I thought you got two so you could share with me," I say teasingly with a smirk, more to keep her from drinking it than the desire to have it for myself.

She licks her lips and smiles. "You want it?"

Goddamn, does she know how she's coming off right now? She's already testing me, because just hearing those words slip between her lips has my dick straining against my zipper. *Yes, I fucking want it.* She's forbidden. The one woman in this city I should stay far away from.

"If you're offering," I answer her with a flirtatiousness I don't recognize. She blushes and tucks her hair back behind her ear. As she pulls her eyes away from me, she catches a glimpse of something across the room that rips the happiness from her in an instant.

I throw back the shot but keep my eyes on her. The cold liquid burns. I was right about it being tequila. It's strong too. Stronger than I expected and it takes the breath from me, making my chest feel tight, but then it relaxes me all the way down.

I hold up two fingers for Patricia. "Another two," I say and stand, sliding the stool I'd been sitting on over to Jules. "I took your shot so it's only fair," I say. Instantly, her eyes come back to me.

I watch as they swirl with a mix of questions. Vulnerability is clearly present and that only makes her that much more enticing.

"I'm not sure I should," she says softly. Her honesty is so raw, so genuine.

"You really shouldn't," I say with complete honesty as well. She deserves that much. She's Little Red Riding Hood in fuck-me heels and I'm worse than the Big Bad Wolf. I lean forward, knowing I'm breaking every rule I have as I bring my lips just inches from the shell of her ear.

Her fingers tighten on the edge of the stool as I whisper, "But you want to. And this is so much better than whatever you were going to do." I'm not sure if what I said is meant more for her or for me, but either way, I've convinced myself.

My rough voice and hot breath make goosebumps trail down her shoulder. Her nipples pebble under her dress, just barely becoming noticeable beneath the expensive fabric that graces her skin. I pull away from her, offering her space and an out.

She could leave if she wanted to. She could walk away. Fuck, she could call me an asshole and I'd sit here and do my best to pretend I'll never go after her again.

It takes a moment for Jules to pull herself together. She sits there in what seems like a daze. It's only when Patricia sets down the shot glasses, spilling just a touch of the chilled tequila, that she meets my gaze again.

I take the one closest to Jules and hold it out to her. She keeps her eyes on me but accepts it.

"Here's to things we know we shouldn't do," I say with a smile, lifting my glass and extending it for a toast.

Slowly, so very slowly, that bit of happiness comes back to her. Her eyes keep flickering with uncertainty to the floor and across the room.

"Here's to doing what makes us happy," she says, forcing her shoulders back straight as she clinks her glass against mine and then downs every drop. She slams her glass on the bar while I'm left holding mine and watching her every move.

I toss it back as she picks up her clutch, obviously ready to pay for the shots.

"Don't." There's more strength in my voice than I should have used. I soften my tone as I tell her, "It's on me." I hesitate then add, "I was just getting ready to leave."

She watches me cautiously, but I look toward the bartender as I get out my wallet. All the while paying attention to Jules in my periphery.

"Well, thank you … what's your name?" she asks.

"Mason," I answer her hoping she's never heard of me, but she brightens and nods her head.

"Thatcher. Yes, I thought I recognized you." She bites the inside of her cheek as something occurs to her and her expression falls slightly. "I'm sorry to hear—"

"To happiness, right?" I say, cutting off her apology, then pass my card to Patricia. It hurts me to say the words, but I don't bother to hide it.

That only makes her frown, somehow making her appear even more beautiful and alluring. We're both in pain. Both getting over something. Only this shit I did to myself whereas she's collateral damage.

She turns to the bar again, the playfulness gone.

"To happiness, and to the things we want," I tell her as I sign the receipt and leave the pen on the bar. I spear my fingers through my hair, feeling the heat of the moment and the buzz of the liquor starting to affect me.

I glance at her and watch as she closes her eyes. It's affecting her too. She's easy prey—beautiful, naive, innocent. I'm an asshole for doing this, but I can't help that I want her. Her eyes haunt me, but her body tempts me.

"I'm going to get out of here." I let my hungry gaze roam down her sexy curves, not hiding what I want from her in the least. "You want to come with?"

Chapter 6

Julia

T*o happiness, and to the things we want.*

Mason's words echo in my ears. I know I'm buzzed, but the odd mix of anxiety and relaxation running through me are from something else. It's the realization that I'm at a crossroads. I'm standing in front of an open door and I know that going through will change everything. It would put my world into motion again, moving me forward, shoving me from the stagnant place I've been in these last few months.

There would be no way to go back, but there's no telling who I'd be once I'm on the other side. My body is ringing with desire and adrenaline.

Mason Thatcher. I've heard of the handsome devil. The

pictures I've seen don't do his broad shoulders and muscular frame justice. The rough stubble on his jaw begs me to reach up and brush my fingertips against it. He's tall, dark and handsome ... and a notorious player. A man I shouldn't be caught dead talking to. My husband would have killed me for having drinks with a man like Mason.

But Jace has left me all alone. And Mason's so much more than I thought I could want in a man.

I rip my eyes from his hard body. Although he's in a suit, I noticed his hands first, rough and callused. It's clear they're from years of hard work, something the men in here know little about. Actual manual labor.

I try to relax and casually lean against the bar, slipping my pointer finger into one of the empty shot glasses and forcing it onto its side. I don't know why and it probably makes me appear drunker than I am, but I don't care.

"Mason, do you like tequila?" I ask him and this time when I speak, there's a bit of flirtatiousness in my voice. Guilt weighs heavily in my chest, but only briefly before the alcohol drifting into my blood numbs the memories. I've been alone for too long. I can have him for a night. Just one night.

Mason's steel gray eyes roam over the curves of my waist and ass. He's bold, licking his lips and then taking a step forward to lean against the bar with me. He's close enough that the heat of his body makes me that much hotter.

I want to know what it would be like for a man like him to

pin me beneath him. To take me how he wants me. I close my eyes as a warm flush rises into my cheeks from the intensity of his stare.

"I do," he replies and his voice is low and rough. It does bad things to me. I rest my head in my hand, both loving and hating the way the alcohol soothes the pain.

This isn't me moving on, but I'm ready to feel something else. My brow pinches at his response when I look back at him, but then I realize he's just answering my question about whether or not he likes tequila. I'm a bit more than tipsy but I'm still here and present, and I know what I want.

Even if I'll hate myself in the morning, it's one night of not going back to that large, empty house alone.

The tight pull of two small hands at my waist and Sue's loud voice make my heart skip a beat and I swear to God I almost scream. I feel like a child caught with her hand in the cookie jar.

"Jules, Jasper's out front." Sue talks like she has no idea she just scared the shit out of me.

My heart pounds in my chest as I turn to face her fully, my eyes darting from the man candy on my right and then back to her.

Caught red-handed.

It takes a moment for me to realize what Sue said, and a moment for her to catch on to what I was about to do.

She eyes Mason but before she can say a word, I say, "Jasper?"

Although it comes out like a question, it's more of a curse.

Sue gives me a sympathetic look as she says, "The exhibition at Ruppert Park must've ended." Jasper's with the *New York Post*. Every time he sees me he has a question and I know whatever I say will end up misquoted in the paper the next morning. He's not kind like the others.

I blow out a heavy breath, looking through the crowd and toward the entrance. I don't feel like dealing with this shit.

"And what are you doing here?" Sue's question is directed at Mason who's standing behind me, still leaning against the bar and resembling sin incarnate. He doesn't seem to mind the interruption at all. He gives Sue a lazy smile that brings back the heat between my thighs full force.

"Just leaving, actually." Jesus, his voice is as smooth as silk.

One split second passes and a wide grin spreads across Sue's face, her dark hair swaying, brushing against her cheek as she knowingly looks between the two of us. I lean backward, gripping the stool behind me and wanting an escape. It's one thing to flirt with the idea of bringing someone home; it's another thing entirely for everyone to know I was thinking about it.

Sue looks pointedly at Mason's cock and raises a brow, which only makes me want to bury my face in my hands.

"Are you ready to go?" I ask Sue and step away from Mason. Gripping my clutch tighter, I'm ready to get the hell out of here. There's not enough tequila in the world to cancel out the sobriety that the mention of Jasper brings me.

"You two get out of here," Sue says, stopping me in my tracks. That's the last thing I expected her to say.

"What'd you say your name was?" she asks Mason.

"Mason Thatcher." He extends a hand to Sue and she takes his hand coyly with both of hers.

"Mason," Sue says and her voice drips with sex appeal. It always does. She's a cold-hearted bitch to some but just as vivacious and insatiable as she was ten years ago when I first met her during my freshman year of college.

She leans in slightly and I get a good look down her blouse. Her necklace shifts so that the thin gold chain and glittering emerald jewel rest on her perky breasts, but when I look up, Mason's only looking into her eyes. "You take good care of my girl tonight, Mason." Sue looks back at me and that roguish look in her eyes makes me smile.

"I plan on it," Mason tells her and releases her hands.

"You are wicked," I whisper to Sue, my smile widening.

"Just one minute," Sue says. She holds up her pointer finger at Mason and grips my wrist, moving me away from him and closer to the powder room as if he can't hear us a whopping twelve inches away. I keep myself from rolling my eyes.

"It's nothing serious." The words sound defensive even to me. I don't want her to judge me or to hate me. I just want her to understand. Out of all the girls, I think she will. More than anything, I know I want to get out of here with a stranger. It makes me feel dirty and shameful, but right now it's what I want.

"Nothing serious?" she says. "It is for me," Sue says. My lungs stall at her words. She shifts her weight and looks over her shoulder toward our booth. I can't see either Kat or Maddie, although I'm sure they're still there. "You need this." Sue stares into my eyes, the look so serious I'm caught off guard.

"The question is," she says as she lowers her voice and leans into me, "are we telling the others?" Oh, thank the good Lord. I let out a breath I didn't know I was holding. When she pulls away, gripping my elbows in her hands and winking at me, I know everything's going to be okay.

I hesitate, glancing back at Mason and then I bite the inside of my cheek. "I don't want to lie to them," I tell her honestly.

"Then you two slip out the back. Do it fast before I go tell them and before Jasper can get his scrawny, organic, vegan-eating ass inside."

I snicker at Sue's response, but the reality of what I'm doing is settling in. I lean forward as Sue lets go and I grip her hand before she can turn and leave me alone with my soon-to-be one-night stand.

"Tell me I'm not a bad person." The words slip out before I can think about what I'm saying. I try to keep the smile on my face, but it wavers.

"Getting laid doesn't make anyone a bad person."

I nod my head, willing the emotions to go back to being

buried deep inside of me as if they don't deserve to surface in this moment.

"Unless he's married," she adds quickly and I chuckle.

The bit of humor helps me feel a sense of relief, but it's small. Her expression softens. "You just need a little something to kick-start your happiness again."

To happiness.

"I do." I nod my head.

True to her nature, Sue ignores the way my voice cracks as she takes a half step closer to me. "Then get over there already. The sooner you leave, the sooner he can be fucking you with your ankles pinned behind your head—"

A laugh escapes me before she can finish. "Can you even put your legs behind your head?"

"For the right man, I can do a lot of things." She looks at Mason, then to me.

"Just have fun tonight," she says, keeping things light but it's calming.

I nod my head as she turns from me, leaving me alone with Mason.

Alone to do bad things and make bad decisions. But at least I'm doing *something*.

Alcohol helps. I can always blame it on the alcohol.

It's then that I notice a few eyes watching. Including Margo, who's taking covert glances. That's when he wraps his arm around my waist and pulls me into him, bringing my back against his front as he whispers in my ear.

"You ready to go?" he asks, his warm breath traveling down my skin and making my body feel alive for the first time in several months.

I don't care that everyone can see. The city can talk; I'll deny it all.

"Will you hold me afterward?" I whisper my one request before I realize what I've said.

His body stills behind me and I close my eyes, hating that I've ruined this before it's even started. It's a one-night stand, nothing more. No emotions.

"Until the morning?" he asks me. My heart beats again, in rhythm with his.

I nod my head, my hair rubbing against his hard chest and his thumb brushing against the black fabric of my dress.

Just until morning.

CHAPTER 7

MASON

Will you hold me afterward?

I'm calm on the outside, as if there's not a damn thing wrong with what I'm doing. I don't know what's come over me.

The Mercedes's alarm beeps as I unlock it and open Jules's door for her. Her heels are muted on the wet pavement as she rounds me and slips easily into the luxurious leather seat. Her soft blue eyes look up at me as she tucks her hair behind her ears and settles the clutch in her lap as she murmurs, "Thank you."

I merely smile and close her door, the keys jingling as I walk to the driver side, my pulse racing wildly.

This is a mistake. I don't hold women afterward. Sex is

sex and nothing else.

But I'm also a selfish prick, and I'd be a liar if I said I didn't want her. What I want, I get.

I start the car, the purr of the engine and soft classical music filling the cabin.

As I look over my shoulder to back out, Jules clears her throat. "Are we going to ..." she starts to ask and then a beautiful blush colors her cheeks.

"Are we going to what?"

With a stronger flush, she shakes her head gently and says, "Never mind ... Of course we are."

I can't help the smirk on my face at her shyness or the way my cock jumps in my pants. I peek at her before leaving the tight parking lot and heading down Second Avenue. My fingers itch to rest against her bare thigh as her dress rides up slightly. I place my hand on the gearshift instead, stopping at a red light and looking over to her.

She squirms in her seat under my gaze and I fucking love it. It's easy to forget with her. Maybe that's what it is. Maybe that's why I can't say no and walk away. If I can just have her for tonight, then it'll all be all right. I'm her downfall and she's my savior.

"Where are we headed, sweetheart? My place?" I give her the option but she's free to suggest someplace else. She's quick to nod, glancing at me then looking down at her hands in her lap.

I'm enjoying this way too much. I turn to look out the driver side window and ignore that voice in the back of my head saying I'm a Grade A prick for doing this to her.

"Thank you," she says softly as the light turns green and traffic starts to move. "For heading out the back and away from all that ..." she pauses, waving her hands in the air before falling back against the seat and concluding, "bullshit."

The curse word seems foreign on those sweet lips of hers. I nod my head once, looking back to the windshield and twisting my hand around the leather steering wheel.

"No problem," I say easily but I can feel her need to talk, to tell me everything else that's on her mind. I wait for it, staring straight ahead, but nothing comes. Just silence as we drive to the sounds of Tchaikovsky.

It's only fifteen minutes to my place at this rate, but the time can't pass quickly enough. Every second of silence is a second I consider turning back. There's still time to walk away.

"Do you always do this?" Jules asks, breaking up the quiet.

"What's that?"

"This," she says, her cheek resting against the seat as she looks at me.

"Hmm?" I still don't understand her question.

"Pick up women—" she stops and rolls her eyes. "You know, one-night stands." Tapping my thumbs on the steering wheel, I consider her question. I used to without thinking twice. But that was before Avery. Before my father and this hell I've been thrown into.

"So I'm right, you do this often?" she says and I have to suppress my smile at her brazen demeanor.

"I'm not going to answer that, Jules." My voice comes out a little harder than I wanted and she shrinks back some. *Smooth, real fucking smooth.*

It's tense for a moment and I flick on the turn signal as we head down a deserted street. So close. I can't lose her now. "I don't take women to my place," I tell her simply. "And it's been a while."

Her brows pinch for a moment and then she struggles to hold back a laugh. It catches me off guard but then I remember how much she drank. I'm still feeling a bit of the tequila myself. My tolerance is high as fuck, so if I'm feeling it, she must be wasted. The realization has me rethinking things again.

"How are you feeling?" I ask her.

"Fine," she says and then covers her mouth with her hand.

"Are you drunk?" She doesn't look like it in the least.

She purses her lips and shakes her head as she says, "Nope. Just right." She stretches in the seat, covering another yawn when I stop at my gates.

I eye her for a moment and then brush it off.

I know Jules comes from money and was born into this lifestyle like me, so I'm surprised to see admiration on her face when we arrive. "Your home is beautiful." Her voice is even and sincere. I'm proud of my home. I built it myself.

Liam, my business partner, helped design it for engineering purposes, but it was all based on my ideas and plans.

I pull up in the driveway as her phone starts vibrating.

She doesn't pay attention as I approach the front of the house. Judging by the look on her face and the way she shoves the phone back into her clutch, her friends from the bar are probably giving her hell.

"Everything all right?" I ask, more to make sure I'm getting her ass into my bed than anything else.

For only a moment, I think she received a message from someone who knows what happened. Someone who saw what I did, although I don't think anyone could have possibly seen. My muscles coil and my knuckles turn white as I grip the gearshift, putting the car into park and searching her face for answers.

She blows a bit of hair out of her face and looks anywhere but at me.

"It's fine," she says but I know she's lying.

"Tell me what's wrong." The command comes out easily.

Her eyes go wide and I almost second-guess talking to her like that. *Almost.* But then she caves to me.

"My friends just found out."

I cock a brow at her. "Found out?" She parts her lips slightly and I'm guessing from the way she leans into me, my touch is all she needs to loosen up. I rest my hand on her thigh, just beneath the hem of her dress, caressing her lightly with my thumb.

"I don't do this often or... ever—"

I lean in and press my lips to hers, stopping her explanation. I move my hand to her cheek and then behind her head as she deepens the kiss. Her lips part for me and her hot tongue massages mine in swift, strong strokes.

I groan into her open mouth, our breath mingling as my dick hardens to fucking stone.

"Forget about them," I tell her as I break the kiss and pull away. She's left breathless, her eyes still closed when I open my door and start to get out, taking the keys with me.

I almost close the door and miss her whispering, "I'll forget about it all."

But I heard her. I heard the whisper, the raw vulnerability and truth in her statement.

I wish I hadn't.

CHAPTER 8

JULIA

I've never had a one-night stand before.

Not once.

It's not like I have a thing against them and Lord knows my friends enjoy them, with or without discretion. It's just never happened. My body heats everywhere, one place a bit more than others when Mason touches me, and especially when he cuts through it all with his demanding ways.

My thoughts race as Mason wraps his hand around my waist and leads me to the front door. The chill in the night air is sobering. I can't explain how my nerves are shooting through me. My breathing comes in a little faster now that the alcohol's all but worn off.

I try to focus on how even our footsteps sound but all I can think about is how I've never done this before.

I'm doing it. I'm going to sleep with a stranger. *I'm going to sleep with someone other than Jace.*

Jace and I met as children, paired up in boarding school. I've never been with anyone else. My heel slips on the paved steps at the thought, almost making me fall, but Mason catches me.

He's quick to grab on to my elbow and waist, his hands hot on my body. It's a shock as something inside of me reacts almost violently to his very touch.

Eight months alone ... even longer since I've been touched. The idea of moving on has never been such a dominating thought, or so terrifying.

I wrap my arms around myself, fueled by both fear and desire. My pulse quickens as I look back over my shoulder and toward his car. Toward an escape.

Mason straightens his shoulders, squaring them and hitting the keys against his leg once. The jingle catches my attention. It's the only sound in the cold dark night.

I stand frozen as I look into his eyes. I'm a fool for doing this. It's not me. Not the woman I am today and not the woman I was before I lost my husband. Mason's steel gray gaze searches my own and I feel lost all over again.

I part my lips, ready to give an excuse, a lie, or even the truth. Anything to just go back in time and avoid being in this situation.

To run, just like I've been doing for the past eight months. Didn't I say I needed a change? I said I needed something drastic, but that was back when the alcohol was flowing and we were surrounded by a crowd of people.

Mason is so very tempting. He's gorgeous and confident, but I can't handle a man like him. I can't deal with this.

Weak and alone. A low whisper from the self-loathing bitch inside of me resonates in my ears. I slam my lips shut without uttering a word, hating that she's right.

I won't leave. I suck in a breath and force myself to be determined. Whether what I'm doing is right or wrong, it doesn't matter. I need a change.

A moment passes with the two of us standing still in front of his porch. Only a handful of steps are between us and his front door. I just have to get there.

My eyes drift from the deep navy door to Mason. I'm caught in place as he takes a single step closer to me. It's only one step, but with it is something powerful. His height, his scent, and his very dominance overwhelm me when he's this close. He radiates desire and my mind may be questioning things, but my body is pulled to him, magnetized by his presence.

It's soothing. Surprisingly so as I let my body move forward, closing the small space between us. He trails a finger down my collarbone lightly, testing my reaction.

"I want to touch you, Jules," he murmurs, forcing my gaze

back to his all-consuming stare. I hadn't imagined it'd be this intense. Not at the bar and not in his Mercedes. He didn't push, and he didn't do anything to make me feel trapped. How odd—now that we're out in the open with no one watching and no enclosed spaces, it's only now that I feel cornered. All because of the way he looks at me.

What's most surprising is that I love it. *I want this.* The way he looks at me is addictive; it's freeing in more ways than one.

I can't wimp out. I won't.

I nod my head once and his fingers trail up my throat. His light touch feels much rougher than he's being with me. I tilt my head as his grip moves to my chin and he just barely brushes his lips against mine. It's a soft kiss that leaves me wanting more. I keep my eyes closed and stay as still as can be when he hovers close and whispers, "I want to kiss you."

"Then kiss me," I whimper, a pathetic plea, or maybe one of strength. My head feels so clouded that it's hard to know what's driving me. Raw, primal instinct or desperation. Perhaps a lethal cocktail of both.

He pulls away just slightly, but I don't let him get far. I take a half step closer to him, my breasts brushing against his shirt and I crash my lips into his. I need him. I need this.

He's quick to wrap his arms around me and pull my body against his. The faint noises of the night surround us and they seem to get louder as my breathing gets heavier. His lips travel down my throat and I throw my head back. I may have been tipsy from the alcohol before but in this moment I'm drunk with lust, and I find it too difficult to care.

"I want to fuck you, Jules," Mason practically growls. He pulls me into him suddenly and forces a gasp from me as he nips my earlobe. "I want to make you cum so hard you forget everything."

I moan as my nipples harden and my back arches. "The only thing you need to worry about is remembering my name," he whispers into my ear, his hands roaming down my waist, stopping at my ass. "Just my name and what I've done to you tonight."

I tilt my head back and everything he's saying is exactly what I need to hear. "Yes," I say into the soft breeze that cools my exposed hot skin.

"Only tonight," he says so low, I nearly miss it. My fingers slip under his shirt so I can feel his bare skin, and it triggers him to pull away from me. Just slightly, only so he can look into my eyes, but I grip him harder. I'm afraid to lose what he's offering me.

I want him. I want his promise.

I want to forget and feel alive again.

"Yes, only tonight," I say in agreement and then press my lips to his, moving a hand to the back of his head. My fingers spear through his thick hair as his tongue strokes mine and he lifts me into his arms by my ass.

I gasp at the sudden movement and wrap my legs around

his waist. He takes the opportunity to trail open-mouth kisses down my neck and torture my deprived body.

I'm sure of it now. All I need is to be held by this man. Fucked by him and ruined by him.

With my back against the wall of his porch, he slides a hand up my dress and between my legs. Petting me, testing me until the sudden spike of pleasure hits me harder than I expected. He presses his thumb against me just right and my grip on him tightens.

I come alive for him, every nerve ending on fire, ready to burst into a flame so hot I can't control myself. He doesn't stop, even as I writhe and beg for him to take me inside. My fingers dig into his shoulders, my nails scratching along his shirt and wishing it were skin.

The pleasure is so intense already. It's nearly too much. I want to pull away because the inevitable drop from this high is going to shatter me. I'm all too aware of it, but I can't help myself.

He never stops kissing me as he balances me in one strong arm and unlocks the door. He never sets me down until he has me on his bed.

And he never gives me the chance to think about anything but the desire threatening to destroy me.

He doesn't take his time with my dress, desperate to have me bared to him. I reach behind me, unclasping my bra as he pulls the lace down my body. His fingers loop around my thong and take it along with the black dress.

My heels fall to the floor with a loud thud. I'm given a quick moment to consider what I'm doing as he pulls his shirt over his head. But instead of giving in to self-doubt, I'm mesmerized by the rippling of his muscles and then by the girth and rigidity of his cock as he shoves off his pants.

It happened so fast. Like a whirlwind of chaos that only surrounded the two of us. The mattress groans with his weight as I prop myself up on my elbows. He slides between my legs, spreading my thighs. My body opens up for him as if he was meant to be there all along. As if my movements are controlled by his desires.

My heart feels like it's trying to get away from me. His hard, hot body pushes down against mine and I can barely breathe.

My head turns to one side and then the other, feeling the cool sheet beneath my cheeks as he brushes against my slick folds.

"You're so wet for me," he says and Mason's voice is a mixture of wonder and reverence. He captures my lips with his and suddenly pushes his cock deep inside of me, all the way to the hilt in one swift stroke.

I scream out, my neck arching and my back bowing as he stills and gives me a moment to adjust to his size. My breath halts in my chest, but then he moves.

Not just moves. He fucks me with a punishing force. The bed slams against the wall with each thrust. He kisses me as though he's breathing the air from my lungs. He pins me down and takes everything from me, forcing me higher and higher, all while giving me everything I never knew I needed.

It's not until I'm left panting and recovering from waves of pleasure that I start to question what I've done. But it's late and I'm so exhausted. I forget it all except his name and what he's done to me, and give in to sleep.

Don't leave me alone, I cried and I screamed.
Don't leave me alone, my whole life demeaned.
You left me unguarded. My heart raw and bleeding.
You left me forever. The pain there left seething.
You left me here weak. Just a stone in the ground.
You left a place beside me, my picture-perfect life unbound.

CHAPTER 9

MASON

Last night was stupid. Such a juvenile word but I can't think of anything better. Fucking stupid.

I'll blame it on the alcohol. A low exhale travels up my throat as I walk away from the floor-to-ceiling window in my office. The hustle and bustle of the street below is what drives me to keep moving. This city never sleeps and the work never ends.

Last night was about taking a moment to unwind from the shitshow my life has become. From my father, the arrogant prick and criminal that he is. The awareness of just how ruthless my father is has never hurt me more.

That's what it really is. *Pain.* Coming to the realization that your father's a disgusting excuse for a human being and should be behind bars is ... difficult to handle. It's even worse when you're tied to his bullshit.

I sink into my leather desk chair and it protests the movement with a groan until I'm comfortable. Unlike my father's office, traditional and smelling of polished wood and old books, my office is the opposite. It's airy and open, modern and sleek. A model of our newest planned development sits in the very center of the space.

That's what started all this shit. A celebration for my company's first suburban development. No more apartments downtown. We're ready to expand into uncharted territories. I'm an idiot for thinking this would change things between my father and me. I really thought things would be different. I'd attributed the tense relationship with him to my own doing. A rebellious child with pent-up anger over his mother's death. Born into this black-tie bullshit.

I was always supposed to act right. Always supposed to say the right thing, stand the right way, behave and pay attention. Well, I didn't want to. I crack my neck remembering the fights I started. A smile kicks up my lips. Four boarding schools and hefty donations from my father still couldn't keep me in line.

Working in construction was just another way to stick it to my father.

Higher education? Fuck that. I got a job ... but it didn't last for long. I'm just not made to work for someone else and I wanted a more physical job. So, I started Gray's Homes with

Liam nearly three years ago. He had the schooling and I had the designs. I didn't think it'd be this successful or grow so quickly. So successful, in fact, that I ran out of capital and so did he. I took out loan after loan, investing in myself and I'd do it all over again. It was worth it to keep growing and taking advantage of the momentum we had.

I should have known better when my father came to me and offered to invest in me too.

Clients were eager to sign contracts with his name on them. Having him back me made bids easier to attain and everything run smoother. I knew it was too good to be true.

He just wanted to be able to hold it over my head. He wanted to *own* me. I narrow my eyes at the model in the center of the room. It's all because of this one project. Now I'm in debt. I owe more than I'm worth and everything is hanging in the balance as we move forward with this one project that I'd love to trash just to spite my father. I should cancel it all now that I know the truth, but that would mean bankruptcy and more people than just myself being affected. Liam and all our employees and contractors. At the thought, there's a sick feeling in the pit of my stomach. One even a night of whiskey and great sex can't dissolve.

I pull my eyes back to the computer screen, back to reviewing all the invoices that have been paid. Everything's moving accordingly and on schedule, but only because of my father's loan.

I run a hand over my face knowing I'm just as much of a fucking prick. I don't deserve to breathe the same air as someone as sweet as Jules.

The thought of her shy smile and innocent looks ... God, it does something to me. The guilt and anger are minimal compared to the desire. I want to feel her again. I want to get lost in her touch and be the one to do the same for her.

I can make it all better.

She has no idea how screwed up this situation is. If my father knew who I'd spent last night with, I imagine I'd never hear the end of it. He may be a piece of shit and deserve to be locked away for the rest of his life, but if the world knew what I'd done, they would think the same of me.

I click the mouse to light up my screen as it goes dim once again. I can't think; I can't focus.

As my temples throb and irritation grows, I think back to last night. Back to Jules.

Out of every possible way for this morning to start, I never guessed she'd sneak out.

I imagined how the morning would go over and over again while I watched her sleep, her long hair a messy halo on the pillow. So peaceful and beautiful.

I couldn't get over how fucked up it was. How selfish. But it was everything I wanted and more. *It was fucking worth it.*

As she slept, exhausted and spent from the raw fuck, my fingers longed to travel along her curves. I was still hard for more.

Staring at her lush lips, the vision of her eyes shut tight, her head thrown back, and her mouth parted with soft, strangled moans spilling between them was etched in my memory. It was the sexiest thing I've ever seen. Jules was utterly in rapture from what I was doing to her. She was completely at my mercy and I know she loved every minute.

I tugged the blankets over myself and lay there watching her, debating how I'd end it in the morning. I could crave her more than anything, but it was over. It should never have started to begin with. As I thought up exactly what to say to ease the sting, I watched her steady breathing and my lungs filled with her sweet scent.

Just once more. I should have woken her up, spread her legs wide and taken her again. Had I known that I'd wake up alone, I would have.

I lean back in my seat, letting out the aggravation in a groan as I watch the security footage again. She slipped out just before dawn, leaving only a note behind. I watch in amusement as she keeps looking up from the pad of small sticky notes she'd found on my kitchen counter. The pen never even touched the paper for a full two minutes as she contemplated what to write.

She's lost and confused. She doesn't even know what she wants.

But I do.

I fidget with the yellow sticky note, passing it from my middle finger to my pointer and back again mindlessly.

Thank you.

If last night was more than just last night …

I trace the delicate, feminine script of the letters. She was made to tempt men. I'm convinced of it. Everything from her soft sighs to the way she carries herself.

It's as if she was designed to lure me in unknowingly.

Even the way she's written her phone number calls to me. Each graceful curve makes my fingers itch to punch in the numbers on my phone.

Weakness. Stupidity.

Last night was a one-time thing. I don't have to call her. I don't owe her anything and I'm sure she doesn't expect a damn thing either.

Why does that bother me even more?

The sticky note moves from finger to finger more rapidly now. I know I shouldn't call her. Nothing good can come from this.

My eyes look back to her message and focus on her phone number.

Selfish. So fucking selfish.

That's the problem, though. I just don't give a damn about anyone else. The thought is what strengthens my resolve. It's all going to come crumbling down around me soon. I deserve to enjoy what little time I have left.

CHAPTER 10

JULIA

Water drips from the spout of the iron faucet. I grip the side of the claw-foot porcelain tub, the water splashing slightly in the silent room as I get comfortable. Then I rest my cheek against the cool hard porcelain and watch the water as it continues to drip.

The water's nearly lukewarm by now, but I don't want to get out. My wet hair clings to my skin as I sink in deeper, letting the water climb to my neck. My legs sway from side to side and I listen to the steady rhythm of the dripping water.

Part of me wants to pretend like last night didn't happen. And this morning—I close my eyes and bring my hands up to my face, embarrassed by the memory. There's nothing in etiquette class about how to leave your one-night stand.

My throat feels raw as I take in a breath, remembering how last night felt. His hands on my body, his chest against mine as he rocked in and out of me, mercilessly, ruthlessly.

I've never ... I swallow thickly, hating that I'm even comparing last night to what I had with my husband. I feel like I've betrayed Jace but I just let myself fall into the water, as if I can wash it all away.

No amount of time spent in this tub will cleanse the sins of last night.

One good thing's come of it, though. The words are flowing through me so easily now. All I've done since I've been home is write. I shouldn't be happy about that; I shouldn't feel like a weight has been lifted, but I do. Every single thing I've written since my husband's passing has been dark and stunted. It's nothing that I would willingly choose to write. My poetry has always been a happy place and now I have a piece of that back.

The pain in my chest though, the way my heart feels tight and my lungs too crushed to breathe, that's because I don't regret it.

I feel guilty that I don't feel guilty. How does that even make sense?

Ping. I groan at the sound, squeezing my eyes tight. I must've been more than a bit tipsy last night to let Sue act as my conscience. She won't leave me alone. There were way too many texts waiting for me this morning for her to have gone home with anyone last night.

I woke up to a myriad of messages.

Please tell me he didn't kill you.

I'm so sorry if he did, though!

Seriously, are you okay? Text me later!

She thinks she's funny. I thought I was doing a good thing by letting her know I was still alive and unharmed, but all that did was open a floodgate of questions.

She's finding more joy in this than I am, which makes me laugh.

I can't help the way my lips beg me to smile and the way my heart flutters. Sue's having a good time teasing me.

Ping. I turn my head to the right, to where my towel and phone are sitting on the marble bench.

I can only imagine what she wants to know this time.

"I can't hide in here forever," I say under my breath, finally lifting myself out of the comfort of the tub. I lean down and pull the plug, letting the cool air hit my heated skin.

It was nice while it lasted and after last night, it did my body good to relax in here. As I lean over to grab the towel, the sensitive bits between my thighs ache again with slight pain. It's a good kind of hurt though, the kind that lets you know you've been properly laid. I laugh slightly into the towel and dry off my body, then work on patting my hair dry. My feet pad softly against the black-and-white penny tile floor.

The bathroom matches the estate's classic interior. Every accent and piece of decor reflect the timing of when the house was built. There are a few modern pieces, but they only accentuate the charm of the classic architecture. It's expensive to maintain, but the beauty is unmatched.

I continue towel-drying my long hair as the memories of renovating the house come to me one by one. The bit of happiness I'd claimed only moments ago vanishes.

Jace and I got into so many fights over this tile. I can see him standing in front of the mirror, glaring at me for being stubborn. It's my family's house, though. This isn't an Anderson estate. I inherited it when my parents moved from the city. We both knew I was far more well-off than he ever was. The steamy glass doesn't hide the past. I can hear his voice; I can see it all like it was just yesterday.

But the memories are from years ago, and he's never coming back.

Ping. This time when the phone goes off, I can't help but want to cling to whatever Sue's said. She could ask how big he is and I'd give her every detail including the veins. I'd be eternally grateful for a distraction right now. I take a seat on the bench, wincing as my sore bottom rests against the hard marble and pick up the damn phone.

It's not her.

Well, this last message isn't.

I have three from Sue, all wanting to know details about

what I did with Mason last night. I roll my eyes and let out a small snort at her question about size. Of course she would ask me. I knew it.

By the looks of him, he should be packing ... but I'm going to guess he's only four inches. Am I right?

She cracks me up. She's been sending me these kinds of messages all day. Anything to get me talking.

Nope, only three, I type back just to give her something to laugh about. She deserves it. Without all these messages and prodding, I'm not sure how I would have handled this on my own.

I click over to the other message and my heart does an odd flip in my chest when I see who it's from. Like it can't function for just a moment. Maybe it's the shock and disbelief, or maybe it's fear? I'm not sure, but either way, I'm struck by the fact that Mason messaged me at all. I was sure that sneaking out would have sealed the deal between the two of us. It was a one-time thing. One I'm grateful for and content with. I knew what I was getting when I went into the arrangement.

I wasn't sure if I should leave my phone number. I imagine he was relieved to find his drunken one-night stand gone and I didn't want him to feel obligated to call me.

At the same time, I hoped he would.

Not because of him. It's not that I'm clinging to having a relationship at all. I just ... I liked the way he made me ... I don't know what the right word is. The way nothing else mattered when I was with him. How it all slipped away and I didn't have to focus on anything but him. Mostly because he was only focused on me.

There's nothing wrong with wanting more of that, is there? I bite down on my bottom lip and read the message.

It's not a hello or an admonishment for leaving him.

I want to see you again. Blue Hill at 8 p.m. tonight.

My lashes flutter a few times as I reread the message. How very presumptuous. As if I have nothing better to do than meet up with him.

I don't, if I'm being honest with myself. I haven't got a single thing to do other than write, which I fell into earlier and loved every second. I lose a little bit of the fight in me at the thought that I am available tonight, but still. This isn't happening like this. I'm not a booty call or whatever he's used to.

I look down at the message again and the second read through only pisses me off.

Maybe I want a good lay too, and by maybe, I mean I really do need it, but I'm not a call girl and I don't want to be treated like one. Last night was something out of my realm.

Sorry. Busy. I type in the words and hit send without even thinking, letting my high and mighty attitude lead me. But as soon as the message pops up on the screen, I wish I could take it back.

My eyes close and my head falls back as I groan in aggravation. I should have just said yes. I mean after all, aren't I using him too? I'm so busy staring at the ceiling and cursing myself that when my phone pings in my hand, I jump slightly.

Are you busy now?

A second passes and then another. Is he toying with me? I think he is. I can just imagine the teasing way he would say it. Like he knows exactly why I responded how I did. I smirk and bite the inside of my cheek as I text back.

Maybe I am

His response is immediate. *No you aren't and I want to see you. Blue Hill at 8 p.m.*

My shoulders stiffen and I can't help but feel like this is some kind of battle of wills. And I have no intention of losing.

I said I was busy.

I wait for his response, a deep crease settling in between my brows.

There's no immediate message back and I start to question my position. I don't want to be alone tonight. I know it's pathetic but I'm so tired of being lonely, lying in bed at night, staring at the other half of the bed where my husband used to sleep.

Maybe I need to take a step back and think this through. Dating isn't exactly an expertise of mine. Neither is hooking up. With a heavy heart I reread the messages and try not to overthink it all, but I'm sure that's exactly what I'm doing.

I contemplate messaging the girls in our group text when

minutes go by and I don't hear from Mason. A lot of pride lives in me, but not when it comes to this. I'm out of my element.

Tossing my phone down, I decide it's probably for the best that I don't see Mason tonight anyway. I've never been alone before and I'm too tempted to cling to him already and overanalyze it all. Pushing my hair back, I wonder if I should try to convince Sue to go out tonight. I'm sure she would if only I asked. Any of the girls would and I love them for it.

The phone pings against the porcelain and I'm quick to read what he's said.

You win. Just tell me when. I'm available for you.

The smile on my face isn't stopped by my teeth sinking into my lip and I sway slightly as I compose my response. The warmth that spreads through me is addictive. It makes me a little too happy, but I'm too caught in the moment to overthink anything else right now.

CHAPTER 11

MASON

"So, who is she?" Liam asks from his office as I'm on my way out. He leans out the doorway, both hands on the doorframe as he smirks at me.

"Who?" I say, turning my back to him so I can lock up my office. It's a habit I've always had. No one else has a key. I've got fifteen employees working here who come and go throughout the day, but my office is only for me.

"The chick you hooked up with last night." I test the doorknob, making sure it's locked and drop my keys into my pocket. I won't be long since I'm only heading out for lunch, which is good because I want to have all these numbers crunched by the time I need to leave for Blue Hill.

When I turn back around, Liam's got his arms crossed and he's leaning against the door, waiting for me like I owe him some sort of explanation.

"None of your damn business," I say, keeping my tone casual and smirking at him.

"Oh shit," he says then lets out a bark of a laugh with a wide grin. "You really did hook up with someone last night?" he asks me with disbelief. Liam's always been a talker. He doesn't seem to mind my demeanor as much as everyone else does. Give him enough time and he can have an entire conversation by himself, so maybe the two of us were meant to be friends.

Pushing off the doorframe he says, "I was going to give you shit for leaving me hanging last night."

"Just didn't want to be alone last night," I tell him honestly. "Better her company than yours," I joke with a grin, trying to lighten the mood even though I want this conversation to be over.

"So, are we going to go over it tonight then?" he asks me.

"Go over what?"

"What our investor said at the meeting you had without me yesterday." By investor, he means my father.

"It wasn't about Gray's Homes." I take a few steps closer to his office. Mine's the largest and in the very back. Liam's is kitty-corner to mine and the only other office in here. Across from his is the boardroom which is currently empty and only ever used for sales pitches and the end of quarter wrap-ups.

"Oh," Liam says and he seems genuinely taken by surprise. His expression lets me know he wants to ask me a million fucking questions, all of which I'm sure I don't want to hear. *Why was my father so persistent on meeting me? Why did he come in here asking for a conference over and over and demanding I sit down with him?*

"It's been a bit rocky between us for the last few months," I say with my voice low enough that it's just the two of us in this conversation. I know Margaret, our secretary, is right down the hall and close enough to hear if we talk loud enough.

"Few months?"

I stare at him, feeling my expression hardening. It was a necessary evil for me to stop talking to my father a while ago. I'm caught between wanting to do what's right and not knowing for sure that I'd be doing the right thing. So instead of taking action, I avoided him every chance I got.

It worked my entire life up until now. Until he told me what I already knew, confirming it and forcing me to face the truth.

"Don't worry about it." I give him a tight smile. "It's got nothing to do with the business."

"And what about you?" he says, pushing further. "I can't be worried about you?"

The simple answer I give him is bullshit and he knows it. "I'm fine."

"Yeah, you keep saying that," he says then turns like he's

going to head back into his office as the phone rings.

"Go get it." I nod toward his office. "I'm just picking up a Reuben from across the street."

"All right." He heads into his office but before I make it another two steps, he's popping his head outside of the door again to ask, "Will you get me a Coke?"

Glancing over my shoulder, I tell him yes as the sounds of everyone else working get louder and louder.

I don't break my stride as I head down the hall. Our company owns this entire floor of the Rising Falls Building; it's a tall office building that's made for businesses just like ours. The second I stepped in here, I knew this was where I wanted to work. There's clear glass everywhere. So much natural light and impressive views of the city to provide constant inspiration.

Even the cubicles have plexiglass walls.

"Out to lunch?" Margaret asks as I stride past her, needing to shake the nagging feelings that wrestle in the pit of my stomach.

"I'll be right back." I nod, again not slowing my pace and head past all my employees to the elevator.

"Yes, sir," Margaret answers with a light-hearted tone. I've never seen that woman not smile. As if being our secretary is the highlight of her day. She's damn good at what she does too. At first, I was opposed to letting someone step in and take control of scheduling and inventory, but as we grew, I just couldn't handle it all.

Pressing the button for the elevator, I try to think about anything other than my father. With the button lighting up, I'm reminded of Jules's text. The irritation and anger nearly vanish.

Just the thought of what was going through her mind when she messaged back makes me smile. She's a testy little thing. I didn't expect that. There's more to Miss Summers than I thought and I'm definitely intrigued.

I check my Rolex as the elevator dings and the doors slowly open. There's no one inside, so I walk right in and hit the button for the ground floor. Only six hours until dinner.

My chest feels tight and the small smile leaves me. It's fucked up in so many ways, but she'll never know. I'll make sure she never finds out.

CHAPTER 12

JULIA

There are pink macarons and crystal chandeliers everywhere I look. I love this place. It's a tiny shop and the treats are far too expensive for what they are, but it's the vibe I truly love. I scoot my silver stool closer to the small round table and unpeel the wrapper on my cupcake as I listen to Suzette.

"I want to know every detail," she says with barely contained joy. Kat glances between the two of us and so far, she hasn't touched a thing on the etched tray in the center of the table. I know there's something there that would make her smile, but she's not interested. I bet she and her husband had another fight. I wish they wouldn't; they love each other. It's been obvious to me since the day she met him.

Clearing my throat, I avoid replying to Sue's comment. I can feel both sets of their eyes on me, but I don't look up. It's too pretty in here to feel this anxious. My eyes settle on the crystal flute of pink champagne and I take a quick sip, tilting my head up to gaze at the carved tin ceiling. Everything in here is pink, silver, shiny and new. So beautiful to look at, but useless in saving me from this conversation.

"How could you not tell us?" Kat's voice is low but not scolding, more surprised than anything. She's still standing with her purse on a stool and I don't think she has any intention of sitting down in the least. Until she does, plopping down with her eyes boring into me. "I want to know who you're seeing," she adds with a pout.

The disappointment in her voice makes my appetite for all things sweet and scrumptious vanish. I knew this was coming. You can't just take off from Katerina Thompson and not have her chew you out later.

"It wasn't meant as an insult," I start to tell her. It's not like I was trying to upset her, she should at least know that for a fact.

"It's because you would have stopped her," Sue interjects before shoving a tiny cupcake into her mouth and biting it right down the middle. She has no shame and gives Kat the answer as if it's obvious. Which it is. If I'm an overthinker, Kat is a second-guesser.

"Of course I would have stopped her." Her wrath is directed

at Sue now and to be honest, I'm grateful. Sue can handle it. She stares Kat right in the eye as she pushes the other half of the cupcake into her mouth with her pointer finger.

Kat justifies her stance. "She was drunk and how many one-night stands have we regretted right after?" She has a point, I'll give her that.

"It's not that I was keeping it from you," I say. There's a small plea in my voice for Kat to calm down. "I was ..."

"You were keeping it from me," Kat says, finishing my sentence for me.

"Only until it was over," I say as my face scrunches with guilt and I hide behind my drink.

"Oh hush," Sue says easily and then nods at me. "Good for you for going out and dusting off those cobwebs." I snort a small laugh and my shoulders shake from it. "He's cute too."

"He'd better be," Kat says beneath her breath, pulling out a bottle of water from her oversized leather hobo bag.

Sue rolls her eyes and says, "You going to track him down and beat the crap out of him if he isn't?" A smile forces its way onto my face and I try to make it go away, but it's not happening. Kat side-eyes Sue for a moment before returning to her water and taking a sip. With that, the tension vanishes. Kat gets why I didn't tell her, I know she does. And I get why she's upset. It's a simple squabble that's over the moment Kat reaches for her own cupcake.

"So, your first one-night stand. How does it feel?" Sue asks.

I could write a whole book on the effects I'm feeling right now. The guilt, the anxiety. But the other things, the bit of liveliness and ... is it pride? Is that what it is? Knowing that I was wanted and desired like *that* by a man like Mason. And that he still wants me. Yeah, that's a bit of pride, which is odd to be feeling over this.

"He texted me this morning." I sway a little in my seat, picking at the hem of the tablecloth. "He wants to go out tonight."

Sue's eyes go wide. "Really?" She grins in slow motion and then makes a face as she wipes her fingertips on her napkin.

"What's that for?" I ask her.

Sue shrugs and says, "Nothing."

"That's not a nothing look," I tell her right back. "That's a something look."

Kat reaches for another cupcake, listening intently.

"You must've been good." Sue pops a piece of macaron into her mouth all the while smiling. The tiered tray was filled with an assortment of sugary treats when Sue arrived, but it's almost empty now except for the large cupcakes.

My mouth opens some and I have to force it back shut. By the heat on my cheeks, I imagine I'm beet red. Yeah, it's definitely pride.

"So, what'd you tell him?" Kat says. "Don't worry, I won't try to stop you," she adds with an asymmetric smile.

I'm embarrassed that I first told him I was busy and then

suggested the exact time and location he said originally when he told me it was my call, so I just cut to the chase. "I said yes."

"You said yes to a date for tonight that was asked today?" Kat asks with a raised brow. Yup, she's just like me.

"I did," I answer slowly as Sue claps her hands and leans her head back with laughter. She's so loud that a few customers in line at the counter look back at her.

"I love her. This is just too good to be true." Sue's smile just gets bigger and bigger until she spots the last tiny cupcake.

"I know how it sounds but I told him no at first, and then he said he was available whenever I was ready."

"So then you said yes." Kat nods her head and I nod in return. I can see the wheels spinning.

"I want to go out and see him again. It's that simple."

Kat hums, her eyes narrowing like she's thinking far too hard, biting her tongue, or both. She finally settles on her response, asking, "So you like him?"

She's awarded another nod from me as I say, "I do. At least I like the way he makes me feel."

There's another hum from her and Sue shakes her head, opting to finish her drink rather than contribute to the conversation.

"You have fun tonight," Sue says with a wink. I give her a small smile back and kiss her cheek before she leaves us so she can get to her meeting on time.

Maddie's not coming to this little cupcake brunch so it's

just me and Kat now. I don't like the feeling that I need armor to have a quick chat with one of my closest friends. I bite the inside of my cheek as I watch Sue leave, the bells hanging above the door ringing as I shift on the stool.

"Kat, look—"

"Nope," she says and holds up her hand. "It's fine. Last night was fine. Tonight is fine." Her eyes are closed as she speaks. She nods her head as if she's convincing herself, moving the purse from on top of her stool to the one Sue was sitting on. She has to shift in her seat to tug down her black pencil skirt. Her white blouse is nearly see-through, but she still resembles the epitome of professionalism. She's always put together and on top of everything.

"I know last night isn't something you would do," I start to say and Kat nods slightly. "I know it upset you for me to leave and not tell you." I lean forward, putting my hand on the table, closer to her.

"I think I overreacted," Kat blurts out before I can say anything else. She doesn't meet my gaze at first, but then she lifts her eyes to mine. "It really is okay, all of it, and I'm not trying to make you feel bad." Her words come out with sincerity and it surprises me how much I needed that. "Or slut-shame you or anything like that. I'm happy that you're happy. I'm just nervous that he's taking advantage of you, or that you're going to get hurt ..." I brace for what I know is coming as she lowers her voice and says, "You know, so soon after everything."

"I know. Thank you." My voice cracks some and I look for my glass, but then find it empty. I run my fingertips down the stem, feeling overwhelmed again with a mix of emotions.

Guilt comes out to play more than the rest. It's not her making me feel guilty. It's the thought that I should still be mourning.

"Am I a bad person?" I ask Kat, finally pulling my eyes from the empty flute to her.

"No," she answers with sad eyes, taking my hand in both of hers. "I didn't mean to make you think that—"

"You didn't," I say and wave her off the path she's going down. "I was just thinking this morning ... about ..." About Jace. I don't say it out loud.

"Just tell me that he's not going to make you miss your deadline." Kat deflects, sidestepping this conversation and creating an out for me. God, I love her. She's my editor and this manuscript is due in two weeks.

A smile grows on my face, but it's not genuine in the least. Not because of Kat or Mason or any of that. It's the use of the word *deadline*. I know for a fact I'm going to miss that deadline. She doesn't need to know that, though. "He won't get in the way of that." I shake my head cheerfully, my hair swishing against my shoulders.

"Okay then," she says as she raises her brows and finally picks up a cupcake. Not the small ones from the tray of random sweets, nope, Kat goes for the largest cupcake with hot pink icing and an Oreo stuck in the center. "Please tell me you're at least using condoms until you get back on the pill or something."

I know she meant for that to be funny, but when I give her a side-eye and a shrug, she practically chokes on that Oreo.

CHAPTER 13

MASON

So close you can touch her,
Delicate and sweet.
You need her, you crave her,
To hide your deceit.
Be gentle and coaxing,
You can't let her know.
If she finds out the truth,
Out the door she will go.

Blue Hill dims the lights in the evening at six o'clock sharp. The dinner atmosphere is romantic with lit candles on the tables, combined with the soothing sound of water flowing down the river rock wall next to the kitchen. The chatter from the other guests goes unheard as I sit here alone. The only sound that resonates with me is the clink of silverware and glasses as I wait for Jules to walk through the doors.

My fingertips brush over the silver tines of my salad fork as I stare straight ahead toward the entrance and maître d'. Multiple guests have arrived since I sat down twenty minutes ago, each one catching my attention and disappointing me. I glance down at my watch again. She still has five minutes until she's late.

I make a habit of being early, but I'm regretting it this time. Every minute that passes makes me more eager to leave. Curiosity is the only thing keeping me here in my seat. The door opens and the soft cadence of heels clicking on the slate floor echoes in the large open space.

She's here. Jules slips her gray wool peacoat off her shoulders when she walks in and drapes it in her arms as she strides to the maître d'. I stand and button my suit jacket as I walk toward her. I'm only a few tables away and she sees me as the man asks her if she has a reservation.

"She's with me." My voice comes out deep, confident ... possessive even. As she turns toward my voice, the hem of her plum-colored dress sways around her thighs. It's tighter around her ass and waist, showing off her curves and reminding me how she looked beneath me last night.

"Of course," the maître d' says and nods.

"Thank you," Jules answers sweetly, giving him a soft smile and looking back at me. It's only a quick glance before a blush rises to her cheeks and she takes my hand.

She has a shy elegance about her, but there's more to her than that. I want to dig a little deeper, if for nothing more than curiosity's sake.

I gesture toward the table, pulling out her chair for her like a gentleman. It's not in my nature, but I have enough manners to impress a woman at least.

"I'm surprised you wanted to see me again," Jules says as I take my own seat. The confession sits between the two of us for a moment as I consider a response.

Before I can say anything, she adds, "Thank you, by the way." Her eyes flicker from mine to the candle. I don't miss how she takes a few glances around us as if she's searching for someone.

I nod my head easily, setting my napkin in my lap and giving her a moment to get comfortable. The waiter quickly pours her a glass of water from the pitcher he's holding.

"Good evening. May I start you off with something to drink?" The young man squares his shoulders and waits, holding the pitcher at attention. He's dressed in a crisp white button-down and dark gray slacks that match his thin tie.

"A bourbon for me, please," I say and wait for Jules. Her slender neck and shoulders are on display. The way the thin straps of her dress lay across the very edge of her shoulders taunt me to pull them down. A simple thin silver necklace sits right in the dip of her collarbone with the word *happy* etched in the middle. It's the only piece of jewelry she's wearing. No ring on her finger. I didn't notice one last night either.

"A glass of chardonnay, please."

"Right away," the waiter says and nods, leaving us alone. Once again, Jules squirms uncomfortably. I love her nervousness and how she has a habit of tucking her hair behind her ear. It only adds to her innocence.

"No tequila?" I say, playing around with her to break the ice.

She huffs a small laugh and rolls her eyes. "No," she says as she unfolds her napkin and moves it to her lap, smoothing it out. "No tequila tonight."

I shrug, waiting for those soft baby blue eyes to look back up at me. "I didn't mind the tequila." I murmur the confession across the table. There's not a damn thing dirty that I've said but she still blushes. There's an attraction between us that's undeniable. It's easy and carefree. But the air is tense as she looks to her left again and then back to me.

She hesitates to say something, then changes her mind and clears her throat as she picks up the menu. She talks without looking at me. "I've never done anything like this."

"Like what?"

"Like, seeing someone."

"Is that what we're doing?" I ask her. "Seeing each other?"

Jules puts her menu down and looks at me with a serious expression. "I have no idea." The sincere answer and complete honesty in her voice force a rough laugh from my chest. I was only teasing her, but she's too sweet and sincere to get a rise out of her.

"You can laugh all you want, but I have no clue what's going on." She picks her menu back up and says, "I'm just along for the ride, Mr. Thatcher."

"Is that so?" I ask her playfully and reach for my glass of water when the waiter returns, setting down my drink first and then hers.

"It is," she says, smiling into her glass and taking a sip of the white wine. She closes her eyes and lets out the softest moan of satisfaction that's barely audible. My cock hardens as I remember last night, the same sweet sound slipping from her lips as I thrust into her over and over again.

She's completely oblivious. Even with a shiver of desire running down my spine, she doesn't seem to notice what she does to me.

"So, what changed in your plans?" I ask as she eyes the menu again. I don't bother looking at mine. I know exactly what I'll have.

A short, feminine laugh makes her shoulders shake as she pulls her long dark hair over her shoulder and then brushes it back again. "I thought this would be better than what I had planned."

Bullshit. I can tell she's lying from a mile away.

"And what did you have planned before?" I say and smirk, pushing for more and wanting to see her admit to this little game she played this morning.

She takes a sip of wine and then answers, "Writing."

"Writing?"

"I like to go to Central Park to write," she says easily, slipping her hands into her lap and leaning forward.

"Are you a journalist?"

"No," she says and shakes her head, "I'm an author." She takes a sip of wine again and I watch as she fiddles with the stem and continues. "I'm not well known or anything. Just poetry." She tries to wave off her insecurity then adds, "It doesn't really make much money, but it's the career I chose."

She's already justifying herself and I don't like it. She should be proud.

"I think that's wonderful. It takes a lot of work and diligence to write a novel of poetry."

Her eyes light up and she visibly relaxes as she says in a delicate voice, "Thank you."

"Who's your favorite poet?" I ask her.

"Robert Frost," she answers quickly. "Hands down."

"I've read a bit of Frost." It's true, albeit years and years ago in grade school and I'm pretty sure I hated every minute I was forced to read it. It doesn't matter, though; my remark makes her calm and that sweet smile comes back.

I clear my throat, smoothing the napkin on my lap and trying to remember what Mrs. Harper said. "'Poetry is when an emotion has found its thought,'" I say as I look into her eyes and try to say the second part correctly, "'and the thought has found words.' I believe it was Frost who said that." Her entire demeanor changes to one of surprise and ease. I'm shocked that I remembered it myself.

A surprised grin looks back at me. It's amazing how something so small can make her genuinely happy. She nods and says, "Yes, I do believe you're right."

The moment between us is filled with comfortable silence as we each take a sip of our drinks.

"So you're in construction, I believe?"

"I'm a developer," I say, hoping she won't ask too many questions. I don't think she has any idea of the connections. I don't intend to lie to her, but I don't need to give her anything that would help her put the pieces together.

"In the city, right?"

"Brooklyn mostly, although we're currently under contract with the city to renovate and rebuild some properties in Manhattan."

"What's that like?"

"Being a developer?" I've never had anyone ask me before and I take a moment to consider my reply. "It's challenging at times and it pisses me off most days. A lot goes wrong and hardly anything goes the way it's planned." I smirk at her as she laughs into her glass at my answer. "Isn't that what all jobs are like, though?"

She nods her head, setting the glass down but then her

expression changes. "I'm not sure I should be doing this," she tells me with her forehead scrunched.

"Doing what?"

"This," she says and gestures between the two of us.

"We're just having dinner."

Her eyes narrow and I ignore the accusatory stare, picking up my bourbon and taking an easy drink of it. It burns just right on the way down, leaving a trail of heat in its wake.

"I just want to feed you," I say in a tone that I hope comes out somewhat innocent.

"And fuck me," she whispers so softly but with a roughness I haven't heard from that sexy voice of hers. I stare into her gorgeous gaze, daring her to blush, to be embarrassed by it, but she only stares back with desire in her baby blue eyes.

"Yes, and fuck you," I say. It doesn't go unnoticed that she clenches her thighs. "You want that, don't you?"

"I'm not sure I should be sleeping with you," she says simply but with a firm resolve in her voice. My heart beats in a way that makes it feel tight. Like there's not quite enough room for it to beat again.

"Are you seeing someone else?" I ask her. My knuckles brush against the white tablecloth as my hands start to fist. I stop them and try to keep my body from showing what I'm really feeling. She better not be fucking anyone else.

She loses the conviction in her voice when she answers, "No."

"Then why shouldn't we?" I say, glancing at the waiter as

he makes his way toward us.

"Because—" Jules stops as soon as she notices him. She plasters on a fake smile that doesn't reach her eyes and waits patiently for him to address her.

"Are you ready for me to take your order?" he asks me but I gesture to Jules, taking another sip to settle my irritation.

"For you, miss?"

"May I have the herb-grilled salmon, please?" She passes the menu to him and rests her hands in her lap, giving him her full attention. Meanwhile, I can't take my eyes off her and wondering why the hell she thinks she shouldn't be seeing me.

"Are the grilled vegetables all right with that?" he asks her.

"Yes, they're perfect."

The waiter scribbles on the notepad in his hand then turns toward me.

"Sirloin, medium rare. Vegetables are fine." I preemptively answer his unasked question, still staring at Jules. The waiter takes the hint, nodding once and immediately leaving us.

"You were saying?" I say, picking up my bourbon.

"I—" Again she hesitates, sensing the change in my temperament. "I don't know if I should really be seeing *anyone*."

I wait for more, taking another sip.

"I'm not sure how to," she says, waving her hand in the air, at a loss for words. "I'm still—" She can't put a sentence together.

"I want to fuck you, Jules. Give me one good reason why

there's a problem with that." I hold her gaze listing all the reasons in my head, but ignoring every last one of them. She needs someone to fuck, to hold her, someone to make her smile. I can do that; I can be that person.

"It's just sex?" she asks and from the look in her eyes, I don't know what answer she wants in return.

Fuck, I wish it were. I can't explain why I want her this badly. It's more than the physical attraction, but I'll never admit the truth to her.

"Just sex," I lie. "If that's what you want."

She licks her lush lips, peering down at her silverware and then up to me. "I'd be using you," she says as if she's confessing a sin.

A bark of a laugh leaves me and my tense muscles relax.

"Use me, Jules." I stare into her blue eyes flecked with silver, feeling the tension between us morph into something sweeter, something darker and depraved. "I want you to."

Chapter 14

Julia

It starts with a kiss.

Then dinners and dates.

It starts with a smile.

Your evenings run late.

It tempts and teases.

And makes you want more.

But it's not how it starts,

When it can only end in war.

There's something about him tonight. Something darker that I didn't see before. It's the way he looks at me like I should be running from him. It both scares me and lures me in.

Lifting the glass to my lips, my one and only glass, I finish off the sweet wine.

"Did you write today?" Mason asks. We've made a bit of small talk and light conversation. I'm still feeling him out. I thought I wanted this thing between us but the air changed a bit ago, and the tension is something else now. Like we're at war, although I don't know why.

"I did, yes." Every bit of it was about Jace, though. Something I'd rather not bring up with Mason. I pick up my glass again, finding it empty and cursing internally.

I head off whatever other questions he has for me by saying, "Why dinner tonight and not just drinks after?" My voice is low, nearly accusatory, but unlike what happened earlier, he doesn't seem to mind.

It takes a moment for him to respond, but he does. "Because I had to eat and so did you."

He takes another bite of his steak and then asks, "Would you rather we were just having drinks tonight?"

"Yes." My answer is immediate. He doesn't seem taken aback. He's calm, unmoving and unbothered.

"Why's that?"

I can't look him in the eyes as my fingers nervously move up and down the silverware. I don't know how to put it out there. "How did you know my name?" I ask him.

"From the papers," Mason says and then quickly takes a sip of his drink.

I nod my head. That's how everyone knows me. "The papers?" I say, hoping he'll elaborate.

"I've read a few things."

"Then you may have me at a disadvantage. The papers know far too much about me," I joke, seemingly innocent, but I'm sure he's aware that I'm prodding.

"That's possible, probable even." He smirks at me, his brilliant smile adding to his charm. I try not to let it affect me, but I'm at his mercy whenever he looks at me like that. I consider the facts and list out all the reasons I have to end this. Maybe the conversation with Kat got to me more than I thought.

I'm vulnerable. *Check.*

I've never done this before. *Check.*

I don't know that I'm okay with this. *Check.*

And a man like Mason could crush me. *Check a thousand times.*

"Well, all I know about you is that you're a bit of a player," I say and dare to hold his gaze.

"I used to be, yes."

"Used to?" There's a tension between us. It's hot to the touch and it makes me want to move closer to him, but I know that I need to keep my distance right now.

"Yes, used to. I mean it. I used to be ... more unattached, then I met someone."

"Oh." I'm surprised by his confession and also by the immediate reaction I have to him meeting someone who made him want to settle down. Maybe all the thoughts and emotions are playing on my face, because Mason continues.

"She's not in the picture anymore and it wasn't anything serious at all." He answers my questions before I have to ask them and I'm grateful for that. "It just changed things for me."

I wish I could keep my expression neutral but I've never been very good at hiding what I'm feeling, and this mix of curiosity and even jealousy surely isn't becoming. "So now you want someone to fuck and take to dinners?"

A deep rough chuckle vibrates up his chest and the way he smiles at me does something to me that makes me reconsider my list of reasons.

"Someone, no." His eyes heat and he licks his bottom lip as he adds, "You, yes."

I huff out a small breath and peer down at my nearly empty plate before looking back up to him.

"I want to take you out, bring you back home and lay you down in my bed." He holds my gaze as he says the words so calmly. I fight the urge to look around the room filled with families and couples to make sure no one's heard us. My body is on fire with the thought of him doing just that, over and over. But the part where he talks about taking me out ... that makes this seem serious. It practically begs for drama, given my history as a socialite. Whatever this is between us ... I don't want that out there for all the judging eyes.

"I feel ..." I trail off as I realize I don't know how I feel, and with that frustration I lay down my silverware.

"What's wrong?"

"I don't really like going out anymore." I blurt out the confession and feel sick to my stomach.

"You don't like going out?" He frowns.

"It just makes me anxious because of something that happened. Something that maybe you read about?" It would be a blessing if he already knew. If he could understand that privacy is an issue for me and this is something I would greatly prefer to keep private.

He stares at me for a moment, although his eyes flash with a knowing look.

I don't want to say it out loud and I wait for him to answer, but he doesn't.

"It's just," I say as my voice gets tight and I choke on the words, but only for a moment, "my husband passed away and it's hard for me to deal with moving on with someone else." I stumble over my next words for a moment when I say, "Because people ..."

"Will read about it in the papers?"

"Yes. It's hard going out and not being with him. That's difficult for me." It feels like a massive weight off my chest to just say it out loud. "I don't know how to handle everyone's expectations. It could go over very poorly."

Mason's next words come out hard, a command if I've ever heard one. "Fuck their expectations."

I'm shocked by how blunt Mason is. I don't think he understands. "I just don't want to be judged—"

"Fuck. Them."

I stare back in disbelief, thinking he can't be serious but he is. His eyes hold an intensity and his hard, muscular arms are corded. He clenches his stubbled jaw and then seems to relax slightly, but I'm still caught off guard. Mostly because I want to obey him. I want to eat up every word he's saying as if it's law and bow down to him.

"You're entitled to feel and do whatever you want. It's no one else's business. Their perception of you is their responsibility. Not yours."

I take a deep breath, hating that he doesn't understand. "Maybe I'm just shallow." I didn't mean to say it out loud, but I did. My breath leaves me and I pick up the empty glass again. Before I have the chance to let out the exasperated sigh begging to choke me, the waiter comes to my rescue, the bottle of chardonnay in his hand.

"Thank you," I say gratefully.

The second the waiter leaves, taking both our plates with him, Mason says, "We can play this however you'd like."

"I don't really want to go out yet. I'm just not ready." I realize he has a point but he doesn't understand that I welcomed these people into my life, and shutting them out now would be like a slap in the face.

"Is it because you loved him?" Mason asks, his forehead wrinkled and his brow furrowed. He can't even look me in the eye. "You loved him and they think you can't move on?

Or that you shouldn't?"

"I loved my husband, but that's not why." I take a sip of wine and staring at the glass I answer, "I just don't know how to not feel guilty about being okay and I'm worried because I don't know how it will be taken."

The words came out easier than I thought they would.

"So you're all right?" Mason asks me and he's so genuine with his concern that I could practically cry.

"Some days are better than others, but it's hard because I wasn't much without him."

Mason takes my hand in his at my comment, squeezing it and opening his mouth to say something, but nothing comes out. I'm surprised at how deep our conversation has gotten.

"I'm sorry," I say, shaking my head and pulling my hand away. "I didn't mean to—"

"Stop apologizing," he tells me in a tone that makes all my worries vanish. "I asked you, remember?"

I nod my head and utter a small response, although I don't remember how the conversation started.

"Tell me something that will make me smile," he says.

A grin plays on my lips at the thought of him smiling and I say, "You're a very handsome man. Very charming. Obviously successful." I lean in slightly and let the tips of my fingers play along his large knuckles as I add, "And I really, really liked last night."

I accomplish my task and sit back in my seat, staring at his handsome face.

"I'm glad you enjoyed it." He keeps his eyes on me as we both sip our drinks. "I would have liked to have had you this morning as well."

I almost choke on my wine but luckily I save myself, swallowing it down and taking a moment to get myself together.

"About that ..."

"I imagine you'll make up for it tomorrow morning." He says it like it's a statement but I hear the question.

Another night with Mason Thatcher.

"I did say I was just along for the ride," I say, reminding him and myself.

CHAPTER 15

MASON

Pretend it didn't happen.

Don't let the truth show.

Curiosity will lead you.

Just where you should go.

She'll lure you and tempt you.

And bid you farewell.

It's only then you'll realize,

You've wound up in hell.

I could blame the first night on shock and alcohol. The second on curiosity. But this pattern of behavior, this deep-seated need to watch her, to touch her, to have her ... there's no fucking excuse for it.

I stare at the computer screen mindlessly. The office is

empty; even Liam's gone home, leaving me here alone with simple tasks that should have already been done.

My to-do list consists of analyzing this inventory and comparing the replacement materials Liam thinks will be suitable. It's crucial to our budget that this works and I need to make the decision today. Every penny is accounted for and spent, all except for this last purchase. All of it for one massive project. And all of it I owe to my father.

It's been hours and I'm purposely dragging my feet. I want all this to stop so I can hit pause. Instead I'm falling down a black pit, forced to make a choice of what will happen when I crash at the bottom.

Sitting forward in my chair, elbows on the desk, I nudge the mouse to my computer and it lights up the screen once again. Two gorgeous blue eyes stare back at me. Her long, thick lashes frame them perfectly. Her skin is flawless, with only a hint of color in her cheeks. But it's her expression that had me staring at her picture all morning. Her lips are parted as if she's about to smile. So close to happiness, but the photo caught her before she could have it.

It's only been two days since I've last seen her, but each night I've felt compelled to message her and make sure I knew where she was. The insecure side of me wanted to ensure she wasn't with someone else. That's the truth of the matter. I trust her when she says she's not involved with anyone. However, I know all too well what loneliness can do to a person and I want her completely to myself.

If I pretend like the events that led to meeting Jules didn't happen, then there isn't a damn thing wrong with what's between us. If only it was that easy to forget.

Knock. Knock.

My gaze lifts to the clock and then moves to the door to my office. It's past 8:00 p.m. and almost time to meet Jules.

"Who is it?" I call out, not knowing who the hell it could be. Maintenance, maybe?

"Your partner in crime." Liam's voice comes from the other side of the door and I relax slightly.

"Come in," I yell out to him, checking my cell phone and seeing a text from Jules. She's waiting for me. The very thought spreads a feeling of warmth through my chest.

I set the phone down, giving Liam my full attention although I have no idea why the fuck he's here.

"You seem preoccupied." Although it's meant as a statement, it comes out as a question. Before I can even think about it, Liam's eyes are on my computer screen.

It's an innocent glance, but he doesn't need to see her. More importantly, he doesn't need to know about my new obsession. I'm quick to exit out of the article about Jules. It was about her husband's passing. How she was dealing with the loss, although the picture they used of her was from years before.

I've read dozens of articles about her over the last few days. They're all the same. Every single one of them ooh and ahh over her. Some articles gush about her charity work. Others are less substantial and concern themselves with her opinion of an event or what clothes she's wearing. They put her on a pedestal and in such a precarious place that it's far too easy for her to crash and burn. And that's just what she did according to the articles that came out after her husband's death.

The sole fucking image I can't get out of my head is one of her crying at her husband's funeral. Maybe they showed mercy by using an older photo for the article I spent the day looking at because on the day she buried him she looked as if she'd died herself.

Inhaling deeply, I will the memory to go away. Wishing I'd never seen that grief on her beautiful face. Wishing I didn't have a hand in causing it.

"Well now," Liam says, ignoring my irritation. "Is this—"

"What are you doing here?" I ask him, cutting him off and leaning back in my chair with my shoulders squared. He's still standing and leaning against the desk casually, but my tone has that arrogant smile on his face vanishing instantly.

He rubs the back of his neck, raising his brow and looking past me out the window as he takes a step back. "I was just wondering if you'd put the final numbers in."

I clear my throat, feeling like an absolute prick. "Sorry, it's been a long day." I rub my shoulders and click on the spreadsheet. "I was just getting ready to put them in."

"So it's all finalized?" Liam asks me with a chipper smile,

seeming to forget that I'm an asshole just like that.

"So far, so good." I force a smile and try to shake off the unease flowing through me. I can't explain the dichotomy of how I think of Jules. I want to take her out, impress her and please her in every way, including showing her off and showing off for her. But I also want this thing between us to be my secret. I don't want anyone close to me to have an idea of what's going on.

It's a design for failure. I can't help what I want, though.

Liam claps once and says, "Perfect." He starts to walk away but then looks back at me with an expression asking if he can pry. Curiosity is evident in his eyes. "That's all I wanted to know."

"You don't need anything else?" I ask him, the beating of my heart raging loudly in my chest. I don't know if I should refuse to answer whatever questions he has about Jules. Everything in me is screaming to deny it all. I can never let anyone know.

"So … Julia Summers?" the prick has the balls to ask me.

Not hiding the irritation by audibly exhaling, I nod in confession. I can't help that I feel a sense of pride as his cocky smile widens.

"It all makes sense now. I guess I can forgive you for being such an irritable fuck lately."

"Watch it," I say under my breath but the smile on my face only encourages him.

"Good for you," he says as he looks back at the screen, but it's only a spreadsheet. "Is it serious?" he asks me and I don't know why. He's never asked me before about who I'm fucking, or dating for that matter.

When I don't answer, he adds, "You just seem unusually preoccupied recently."

I move my seat closer to the desk, stretching my back and then shrug, doing my best to come off casual. "I've had a lot on my mind."

He waits for a moment, expecting more, but I return to the spreadsheet and open the folder of options on my desk. "I'll have it done before I leave," I tell him, giving him a tight smile and ending the conversation.

He leaves quietly, merely waving a goodbye on his way out and letting the door shut with a loud click that fills the empty room.

I look up when he's gone and tap the pen against the desk. I don't know what to deny and what to keep a secret. Confusing the two could be fatal, but the lines are already blurred.

CHAPTER 16

JULIA

This is not a date.

This is not serious.

This isn't something that needs to be more.

This is for fun.

This is pretend.

My pen stops on the last line. I stare at the words I've scribbled into the notepad, but my mind is blank. I don't know what I intended for this poem to be. Inspirational maybe?

It all just looks like lies to me.

I click the end of my pen over and over. *Click. Click. Click. Click.* Debating ripping this sheet out of the notebook and balling it up for the round cabinet ... a.k.a. the wastebasket.

The clink of several ceramic mugs being stacked together

makes me turn to look over my shoulder. I inhale the rich smell of coffee in the small shop. The floors are checkered and the walls painted plain white, but this place serves the best coffee downtown. It's also right across from Mason's office and I told him I'd meet him here. My eyes drift up, my thumb still on the end of my pen.

The Rising Falls Building is sleek and modern. It looks like a polished black sheet of glass all the way up with a thick steel frame outlining everything in matte black, separating the panels. It's tall and dominating, dwarfing the small buildings across from it.

It's everything Mason is. The clicking stops when I drop the pen.

With both hands wrapped around the mug, I pick up my coffee and take a sip. It's not hot anymore, but it's not room temperature either. The smooth ceramic feels just right in my hand as I take in a deep breath.

I keep telling myself I shouldn't be with him; I don't do casual and never have, but this doesn't feel casual. It's been days of seeing him and I'm already catching feelings. Feelings I'm certain are one sided.

Maybe I'm reading into things too much. It's only been a week and a half. It's just sex ... or so I keep telling myself. *Maybe I should add that to the list of lies in my notepad.* I huff at the snide thought.

Luckily, not many people have seemed to notice, other

than Kat checking up on me and gently prodding. That's not atypical for her.

We aren't seeing each other in public, mostly. Not for events anyway.

There are whispers that I'm dating, but nothing that seems malicious or judgmental. Which is better than I'd hoped.

My heart pounds painfully in my chest at the thought and the small air of confidence leaves me. I would care if they said I was a bitch for moving on too soon. Or that I'm no longer the good girl they thought I was. That Jace's death was in some ways my death too. They wouldn't be wrong about that last one.

Most importantly though, I don't want Jace's father seeing that I've moved on. Or my mother. I close my eyes and try to rid myself of the image of her reading about me in the paper as she sips her morning tea. Drunk at a bar with a known player holding me. Yeah, I don't need my mother seeing that.

The bells above the front door jingle and my eyes instinctively open at the sound.

There he is, Mason, taking the breath in my lungs as he strides toward me. I'm stuck as I sit there, pinned to my seat and captivated by the air of confidence he gives off. His steel gray eyes look darker than ever as he grabs the back of the chair across from me and pulls it out. The legs scrape on the floor, announcing to the world that he's going to sit with me. He claims his seat and fixes those eyes on me.

"Jules," he says, my name falling from his gorgeous lips in a rough baritone and I finally breathe.

"Mason." I say then smile, although I don't know why. I simply can't help it. He makes me feel like a little girl caught in a fantasy. It's the way he wears his suits, the way he walks into buildings, the way he looks at me. As if he owns them all.

A small smile plays on his lips as well. I did that. I made him smile. These feelings, this bubbly laugh that erupts from my lips as I take a sip of my coffee ... this is where the real problem hides.

He gestures to my cup and asks, "Should I get one as well?"

I sit up straighter and look over my shoulder again at the counter with the one lonely register and stacks and stacks of mugs behind it. It's late but this coffee shop never closes, because this city never sleeps.

"If you'd like to." I don't expect him to reach across the table and tuck a strand of hair behind my ear. His eyes and hands linger on the exposed part of my neck. The tips of his fingers trail down my skin slowly, with purpose. I feel the heat race through me, the desire creeping slowly down my chest and lower ... and lower. He confuses me when I'm near him. I can't think of anything but what I want him to do to me and that's a dangerous thing.

I'm mesmerized by the way he looks at me. The steel gray seems softer, the harsh lines of his jaw less intimidating, more vulnerable. Maybe my poetic mind is getting the best of me.

"I think if I do," he finally answers, leaning back in the chair he's claimed as a throne, "I'd like to get it to go."

Nodding vigorously, I make it obvious that I agree and then feel foolish as he lets out a rough laugh. The bells jingle again in the doorway just as he leans across the table for a kiss.

Anxiety shoots through me, and I pull back just as his scorching hot lips touch mine. My back hits the hard plastic of the chair and my eyes whip over to an old man in a tweed suit. His white hair looks ruffled from the wind, but he doesn't seem to care. His light blue eyes gaze through horn-rimmed glasses and up at the menu behind me.

I'm slightly relieved that it wasn't anyone who would recognize us, but that doesn't last long. My heart drops when I see the expression on his face.

It's more than disappointment; this is something else.

"I don't know ..." I say but trail off, clearing my throat. I'm still trying to catch my breath and explain when Mason speaks before I can continue.

"If you're with me," he says and the tone Mason gives me is authoritative as his eyes pierce me, pinning me to my seat and stealing my excuses from the tip of my tongue, "then you're *with me*." He finishes his thought and I can't look away, I can't shake off this guilt.

"You know I prefer discretion," I say and the excuse leaves me in a single breath.

He rises from his seat and buttons his suit jacket. The

hold he has on me is finally broken although he doesn't look at me as he walks past me and up to the counter. I stare at the door, wondering if I should just leave. My body feels hot and I don't think I can do this. I still don't even know what *this* is.

It's definitely not "just sex." Going out on dates and coffee meetups aren't in the fuck buddy handbook. Not according to Sue, anyway.

My body stands on its own. Although my legs feel wobbly, my body weak and my head clouded with frustration and confusion, something inside me pushes me forward. It's only four steps, four strides toward him, all the while my heart beats faster.

"I don't know what *this* is." My voice comes out strong, clear and full of a confidence I don't possess.

A shaky breath comes and goes as he faces me, his shoulders squared, to give me his full attention. I try to come up with the right words. "I don't know what I want." The words are so true. "I am not *with* anyone. I'm alone and that's—" I stop midsentence.

I almost say that's how I want it. I almost lie to both him and myself.

From the corner of my eye, I notice the barista who looks away casually as if she wasn't listening. My cheeks flame with embarrassment.

"If you want me to leave you alone, it's done." His statement lacks both conviction and emotion.

"I want you," I whisper, my eyes pleading with his. "I just don't," I say then swallow and force my eyes to meet his. "I don't want people to know."

I feel like an asshole. "I'm not ashamed of you ... I'm ashamed of me ..." Oh God, even I cringe at my words. It's the truth, but it's so shitty of me. I swallow thickly, searching Mason's face for something. For understanding or anger. For something, anything. Instead there's a coldness that greets me and it hurts. "I don't mean it to come out in a way that is offensive. I've just been thinking a lot about it since the other night and I don't want my family to find out." My voice breaks at the last statement and that's when the barista decides to set down Mason's coffee.

"It's because of your husband?" he finally asks me and I don't waste a second to answer yes. The word is barely a breath. It's more than just publicity and articles that paint me however they want. It all cuts deeper than that.

"I want to take you home," he says then licks his lips, and instinctively my eyes are drawn toward them. He lets his eyes roam down my body. "We can talk about this in bed."

My lips part and I struggle not to look back at the barista who's no doubt watching us.

"Do you want that, Jules?"

I do. I want him to touch me and hold me and make me feel alive.

Why is this so hard? It's emotions, that's why. Luring me

in and then snapping me out of it.

"Jules?" he asks, pushing me and I cave to what I really want, because if I deny him, I may lose this chance at an escape forever.

"Yes." I whisper my response and I hope the tone reflects my gratitude.

I think it does because he places his hand on the small of my back, as if he knows I need support in this, leading me away from the counter and toward my jacket and coffee that I've left on the table.

As I pick up the white jean jacket, focused on calming down and ignoring my overactive brain, Mason leans forward and whispers in the crook of my neck, "I don't know what I want, other than I want you in my bed every night." *Every night.* There's a pang of both fear and desire from his confession. A small wave of relief and arousal flood through my veins. He lifts the jacket over my shoulders, helping me slip it in place and then looks me in the eyes.

"Is that something you want?"

That's what I want, but this seems like more. I choke on the answer, the words colliding together in a jumble and refusing to come out.

It's because I don't know how to separate the two. A relationship versus someone to sleep with at night.

It's going to be a problem for me, I already know it is, but telling Mason that in this moment is something I can't do. If

I do, I've lost him.

Silence sits between us for a moment, growing more tense by the second and as though it slows the clock in the room, time stalling and my mind whirling with how this is all going to end.

He's going to crush me. He'll leave me shattered when he's done.

He's not the first though and there's not much of me that can break any more than I already have.

I put a small smile on my face and nod, feeling as though I'm making a death wish. "Yes," I answer, holding his gray eyes, "I want that too."

He doesn't know the truth and I'm too much of a coward to tell him.

I've sealed my own fate in this moment. I know I have.

If only I hadn't said it. If only I could walk away.

CHAPTER 17

MASON

What's right and what's wrong are overrated.
The lines are blurred; consequences negated.
I'm left with no truth, only lies that I've built.
I'm left all alone, consumed by the guilt.

She's fidgety, quiet too. My parking spot is the last one on this level in the garage; it's the largest and away from everyone else's. We walk in unison, my hand still on the small of her back. I'm not letting go until I have her in my car. She's running, we both know it, and I won't fucking allow it.

She needs to know that she belongs to me. She wants to hide this and that's fine with me. But only to the extent that she knows not to be ashamed for going after what she wants. Discretion is one thing but I won't be denied.

I'll give her everything she desires; I want to. I want to see her smile, to hear that laugh that drew me to her. I'll do everything I can to make it up to her.

And she'll give me all of her in return. There's no exception to this compromise.

The passenger side door clicks loudly in the empty garage as I open it but then I stop, shutting it before she has a chance to slip in.

My dick is hard; my blood is hot. Glancing at a confused Jules, her doe eyes stare back at me. The same eyes I've been looking at all day. But there's no hint of a smile, only concern and rejection mixed in those soft blue hues.

There's a large cement post to the right of my car. It's square in shape and maybe three feet wide. If someone drove up, it would block us for the moment. Only a moment, but the odds of anyone coming to a commercial parking garage this late at night are slim. Fixing what's between us right now is worth taking the risk of being caught.

My shoulders are tense as I slip off my jacket and lead her to the front of the car, where we'll be blocked from view. Her heels click and her eyes flicker with a knowing want. Although her steps are hesitant, she follows my lead, looking over her shoulder and no doubt wondering what exactly I have planned for her.

"Mason?" The hesitation in her voice comes out as a gasp as her lush ass presses against the car.

My only answer is to grip her hips and back her up to the hood of my car, pinning her down and crushing my lips against hers. Her hands fly to my chest pushing me away at first, caught off guard by the sudden change of plans. But then they travel up my neck ever so slowly, giving in to me and then move to the back of my head, pulling me in for more.

That's a good girl. My good girl. The woman who needs me and I damn well need to show her I need her too.

I break our heated kiss to breathe, her chest touching mine as I look down at her. "Be good for me and be quiet." I murmur the command and she can only nod in response, her warm breath trailing down my neck.

I crush my lips to hers again and she moans into my mouth, but before she can deepen it, I fist her hair in my hands. Pulling her away, I grab her hip and flip her over so her breasts are pressed against the metal.

"Stick your ass out for me," I command her in a rough voice as I palm my dick through my pants and look around the pillar. There's no one in sight and I fucking need her tight pussy coming on my dick.

Her lust-filled whimpers encourage me as I pull her head back by her hair and kiss her neck. She rocks her hips and that small space between her thighs brushes against my dick. Teasing me.

I'm quick to unzip my pants, my pulse racing from the very thought that someone could see us or hear us. I finally let her go to stroke myself once and wait for her reaction now that she's fully aware of what I plan to do. She lets out a gasp, bracing herself and looking over her slender shoulder at me with those gorgeous blue eyes so full of lust ... and trust.

Slipping her lacy panties to the side, I kiss her neck once more before shoving myself deep inside her tight cunt. *Fuck.* She feels too good. With my eyes closed, I give her a moment to adjust. Only for a moment. This has to be quick, no time for playing.

Her back arches and her fingers scrape along the car, but she doesn't scream out. Nothing leaves her lips but a small gasp as her mouth forms a perfect O. Her pussy spasms and feels like heaven as I hold in a groan and place my hand on the small of her back, pressing her down and keeping her in place.

Her eyes are closed tight and her teeth sunk into her bottom lip. I rock out slightly and push back in, forcing the sweetest sound from those beautiful bloodred lips. A moan of pleasure.

I grip her chin in my hand and force her to look at me. I want her to watch me. I want her eyes on mine as I take her just how she needs.

Her eyes slowly open as she lets out a breath and that's when I slam into her again. She bucks forward, a small cry uttering from her lips and I wait again for her to look back at me.

"You need to watch me, sweetheart," I say with an even voice even though it's really a demand.

I'll show her who she belongs to and how good I'll be to her. But she has to watch me, she needs to see it all and know this is exactly what she wanted. *That she wanted me.*

She rests her cheek against the car and keeps her eyes on me as I thrust into her again and again, pulling all the way out and then slamming all the way back in. It's difficult to keep the groans low but I do, and she does what she's told, staying quiet and watching me as I fuck her like she deserves to be fucked.

The sound of tires squealing above us makes her squirm beneath me, but I hush her and lower myself closer to her. Leaning down, I push my chest against her back and kiss her gently on the lips. "They won't see." My hand slips between us and lifts up the front of her dress, lightly running along her clit.

I play with her, teasing and rubbing while watching her writhe under me. "Look at me," I command her and she's quick to turn her eyes to me. They reflect nothing but torturous pleasure and the need to cry out her release. She's gorgeous and I could make this easy for her. I really could. I could fuck her quickly and take her over the edge so she doesn't have to fight the urge for long. I could let her close her eyes and look away.

But I'm not interested in that.

Jules is going to see. I won't let her think this is all pretend and something that it's not.

I'm going to give her everything she needs. I'm going to make it all right again and she's going to love me for it. I couldn't care less if that makes me a prick.

It doesn't matter how it's going to end, just that it happens this way. Right here and right now.

"Mason." She whispers my name as her release takes her gently, her soft folds taking me deeper into her. I have to wait for her to stop trembling, a cold sweat breaking out along my skin before moving my fingers to her lips. I wish she were naked so I could see every inch of her. So I could see the flush that's creeping up her chest.

"Turn around." I give her the simple command and she obeys, her chest rising and falling unsteadily and her legs still trembling slightly.

"This is going to be quick," I tell her and then grab her hips in both my hands and angle her how I want her. I glance up to make sure she's still watching and just like the good girl she is, those gorgeous pale blue eyes are on me. I piston my hips, surprising her as she braces her limp body against the car. The intensity of the raw fuck makes her bottom lip drop with a silent scream as her body tightens. I fist her hair again and pull her head back.

"Mason." My name is a twisted word of desperation on her lips.

"Come for me," I tell her, moving my other hand to her clit again to strum her swollen nub.

She screams out for the first time and I'm quick to bite her neck. Hard. It's a punishment for not obeying me and it only makes her struggle against me harder. And only makes her impending release that much more intense.

I fucking love it. I love what I do to her and how much pleasure it gives her. How she makes me forget everything when we're together like this.

Her body goes rigid and her pussy tightens around my cock. She struggles to breathe and her head falls back as she looks at the cement ceiling, her climax threatening to crash through her.

I nip her chin and move the hand that was gripping her hair to her face. I stare into her eyes as her body shudders and her neck arches, her hair draping over my shoulder. Her face is the epitome of sinful ecstasy. It's the most beautiful thing I've ever seen.

"Fuck," I groan as she finds her release. It only takes four more thrusts, riding through her orgasm and taking her that much higher until I find my own release. My balls draw up and my spine tingles. I bury my head in her neck as my cock pulses deep inside of her.

The sounds of our heavy breathing surround us for a long moment.

I kiss the side of her neck right where she's marked from my bite, running my nose along her soft skin and breathing in her scent. Her legs are still shaking and a shudder runs down her body as I pull my lips away from her. She's perfectly sated, just as she should be.

"You're mine, Jules," I murmur but make sure it's loud enough for her to hear and watch for her reaction. Her long lashes flutter as she opens her eyes and looks back at me. I pull her panties back into place and fix her dress.

"Mason," she says, whispering my name as her forehead creases and her eyes beg me to take it back.

"No, you want me and I want you. You're mine."

She bites down on her bottom lip and says, "I'm not okay." Her voice hitches and her words crack. She closes her eyes and speaks as if it truly pains her to say the words. "I don't know if I can be good for you."

I rest my forehead against hers and ask her, "Why are you so afraid?"

"I don't think this can just be sex for me," she says. I cup her jaw in my hand and brush my thumb across her cheek. "I think I'm going to want more. I think I already—" she stops as her voice cracks again.

My body feels unbearably tense, each breath hurting my chest. *Why am I doing this to her? Why can't I just let her go?* Because I'm a selfish prick and I can't help myself. "I can give you more," I whisper in the air between us, knowing it's what she wants to hear. "We can see how it works between us in private, and keep things quiet in public?"

I'm giving her exactly what she wants, just to keep her.

I'm an asshole for doing it, knowing I can never be what she really needs and wants.

Her eyes light up and that soft smile reappears on her face. She brightens with hope and my shy girl comes back to me. "Are you sure?" she says, still panting, barely recovered from what I've already done to her. "You aren't going to break my heart?"

She has no idea that she should be running from me. I'm well aware that I should turn her away regardless. Instead I smile down at her and kiss the tip of her nose. "I'm sure," I tell her and hate myself that much more.

CHAPTER 18

JULIA

There's no rhyme or reason for when the memories come back. There's nothing I can pinpoint that triggers it. Nothing that I can blame.

Lying in Mason's arms, naked and warm, the two of us each working on our laptops in comfortable silence, there's not a damn reason that I should be thinking of Jace, but I am.

I don't want to. Even as I scoot my back close to the sofa, I try to rid myself of the images of him smiling at me. When I'd wake up in the morning, Jace would push the hair from my face and give me a quick kiss. Always on the lips, no matter how much I tried to dodge them. He thought it was cute how I didn't want him to smell my morning breath.

Moments like that, moments we shared together that were easy and fun, where we fit beautifully together, those hurt the most when I remember. I let out an uneasy sigh and try to relax, ignoring Mason's eyes on me.

You'd think I'd be happy that I had that at one point in time. That I had a man who loved me and whom I loved too. It's easy to say: *I'll be glad because it happened and not sad because it's over.* But the truth is I can't say that, because I don't mean it.

"What's wrong?" Mason's deep voice cutting through the silent evening makes me feel even worse. I'm trying to move on, but it's not that easy.

I swallow the lump in my throat and pull the dark gray throw over my legs and up to my shoulders. "Just having a moment," I answer honestly, although I can't look him in the eye. I hope he'll just let it go.

His warm breath surrounds me as he pulls me closer to him and kisses my hair. I don't expect the gentle touch from him. He whispers, "I get it."

He splays his hand on my hip and runs his thumb back and forth over my bare skin. I wait for more, but he doesn't say anything else. Only that he gets it and my treacherous heart thumps in recognition.

My laptop jostles across my legs as I try to get closer to him, loving the warmth, needing more of it. I wonder if it's wrong to be upset over the passing of your husband while in the arms of your lover.

"Sometimes—" Mason starts to speak just as my eyes glaze over and the words on the screen start to blur. I take in a steadying breath and stop that shit. Crying never helped me. It doesn't do any good at all.

Mason clears his throat while I wipe under my eyes.

"When my mom died, sometimes it was the oddest things that set me off." I'm surprised by Mason's confession and grateful to be talking about him and not me.

"I'm sorry about your mom." My condolence is softly spoken; my voice a bit scratchier than I'd like. I stare up into his eyes which appear so much lighter than usual, maybe because it's dark all around us. Only the glow of our laptops and the city lights beyond the large living room window to paint the room in a soft glow.

He tilts his head to the side, tucking my hair behind my ear and I push my cheek into his palm. He has such large hands, rough but warm. They're the perfect size for this.

A coarse hum comes from deep in his chest. It's short, but a sound of approval.

"It's okay to hurt still." His words are comforting. "It's okay to cry and let it out, even if you're already spent."

My heart beats harder and my breathing becomes more difficult with every passing second that I absorb his statement. I search his eyes for something and he must see the panic in mine.

"Or we can do something else?" he says.

"Like what?" I ask him.

He clicks his tongue, his gaze on my face, but not my eyes. Finally, he takes his hand away and types something into the search bar on his computer.

He pulls up a book of poetry. Robert Frost.

I eye him curiously and he pets my hair before pulling my head closer to rest on his shoulder. I get comfortable as he says, "I can read to you?"

My heart hurts so much in this moment. Not the pain of what I've lost, but the pain that I have something so beautiful and something I'm so grateful for, and yet I still have these moments.

I nod against his shoulder and say, "Please."

I could listen to his deep, rugged voice read poetry to me in the dark for hours.

I could rest in his warm embrace for days.

I could stay here with this man forever.

CHAPTER 19

MASON

It wasn't supposed to be like this. It wasn't supposed to be this much more. Two weeks have passed and it's all become more and more normal. More and more it feels like I've finally won her over.

I watch Jules as she licks ice cream from her spoon, her tongue flat against the bottom and mindlessly watches the news. Her notepad is in her lap with the pen on top although she was writing when I walked in here. It's 4:00 a.m. and she can't sleep.

My mother used to feed me ice cream every night before bed. I had to be in my room and under the sheets as soon as I was finished, but I got ice cream every night. She made sure to keep a variety of flavors on hand; I wanted something different every night. Mom always ate strawberry, though. It was her favorite.

Jules glances over at me, a flirtatious look in her eyes. "Do you want some?" she asks, maneuvering her body in catlike motions to crawl over to me.

Even though I shake my head, there's a small smile on my lips as I wrap my arm around her and place my hand on her thigh to scoot her closer to me.

She moans softly as she scoops up a bit of cherry ice cream from the bowl. That move has to be intentional but her gaze stays on the television as if it's not. Maneuvering on the sofa, I readjust myself in my pajama pants.

She peeks at me, blushing and then brushes her arm against my bare chest.

"You're sweet to get me this," she says with that look in her eyes. The look that tells me I've made her happier than she thought she would be. "Thank you," she adds and plants a small kiss on my shoulder.

Staying up to distract her wasn't my intention when I came out here, but I don't mind. Truthfully, I couldn't sleep either. I felt the absence of her warmth the moment she got up. For such a graceful woman, she's not very quiet getting out of bed.

I gave her a few minutes to see what she would do, peeking in the doorway to the living room as she got lost in her words. Watching as she sat cross-legged on the sofa, leaning over her notepad and scribbling like mad. It wasn't until she started to cry that I came into the room. I thought she needed me; I thought it was about him.

But she said they were happy tears, like the kind you cry when you've gotten closure. I don't know why that hurts me more.

"No problem, I wanted to get out anyway."

"Did you go for a run?" she asks me, eating the last of the ice cream and facing me. I shake my head no. I don't have time for that right now. Usually she's in bed when I run early in the morning and then shower before she's gotten up. It's been a week of her staying at my place and that being the routine.

"My fault?" she asks and scrunches her nose, not liking that she's thrown off my schedule.

"It doesn't matter," I tell her. It truly doesn't. "I'll make it up later tonight."

She hums a small sound and then adjusts on the sofa. "Will you come by my place tonight? Instead of here?"

I answer easily, not thinking twice, "Of course. I may be late; I have a lot of things to wrap up at the office."

She straddles me then, a leg on either side of my hips until she settles into my lap. I let my hands rest on her ass as she drops the empty bowl and spoon beside us on the sofa, the spoon clinking as she shoves them farther away.

"Mr. Thatcher," she says as she wraps her arms around my neck and squares her shoulders. "You're going to be late. I need you to stay at the office ... and help me ..." Her long

lashes flutter as she bites down on her lip and continues, "...
to file the paperwork."

An asymmetric grin finds its way to my lips as she laughs
at her own attempt to be a sultry secretary. I can tell she's
holding it in, not taking it too seriously at all. Her straddling
me though, that has nothing to do with role play.

Glancing at the clock behind her, I note that I have
another hour at least before I need to get going. "I think you
may be mistaken, sweetheart," I tell her.

She rocks herself against me and gives me a smoldering
look. It's one I don't get often, one full of confidence and
determination. But damn, when she does give it to me, it
drives me wild. If anything, this woman knows what she
wants and with the tension gone between us, she wants me.

"You need your exercise, Mr. Thatcher." She drops her
voice low and slides the straps to her silk nightgown off her
creamy shoulders, exposing her breasts. They're small but fit
perfectly in my hand.

With a groan and another rock of her hips, my dick stirs
in my pants and I sit back on the sofa, thrusting my hips once
and making her gasp as she reaches out to steady herself by
clinging to me.

My hands wrap around her small waist as she kisses my
jaw. I don't know when it happened, but my control has
waned with Jules. I love it.

This is such a fucking mess. A beautiful mess.

CHAPTER 20

JULIA

Happy is relative.

An emotion in time.

Guilt waits in shadows,

Makes you pay for your crime.

When push comes to shove,

And the two have to meet.

You'll be judged, never loved.

It's all bittersweet.

I breathe in the steam of the hot coffee in my hands. It's the most amazing smell this early in the morning. That or Mason's pillow. I don't know what it is about the masculine way he smells that drives me crazy. Each morning I pull his pillow out from under him and take it as his alarm goes off.

I can't stop the smile that spreads across my face remembering this morning how he flipped me over and "punished" me for it. Maybe things are moving along too fast, but for the first time in a long time, I'm happy. Genuinely happy.

"Stop smiling like that," Maddie playfully scolds from across the table as she blows on her latte. She lifts the cup to her lips and eyes me before taking a sip. The smile doesn't fade; her next comment only makes it grow larger. "You're making me jealous."

"That is the power of sex," Sue says as she takes her seat across from me. Her coffee is in a to-go cup in her hand, so I imagine she'll be leaving shortly. She sets her bag on the floor and slips onto the stool easily. "It's about time you girls caught on and decided to get some." A coy smile lifts up the corners of her lips as she adds, "Well, except for Kat since she's married."

Maddie laughs into her cup and Kat gives Sue a cold look for a moment then shrugs. "He's good at what he does," Kat says but we all know there have been some complaints recently in that department. Not the bedroom per se but the lack of anything happening in the bedroom.

Whenever Kat looks at me, it takes me down from this high. She represents what I once had and what I should really be striving for. She has a loving husband, a stable and growing career. Children are in her future. I know they'll get over this hump. She loves him and he loves her. Every marriage goes through ups and downs. That's what everyone told me when

Jace and I were working out our problems.

I set the cup down on the table and try to stop being ... whatever it is that's come over me.

"Is it different?" Maddie asks me as she crumples the wrapper from Kat's straw. She has both hands on it, balling up the small white paper into a perfect circle. "Like since you were only with Jace before this new guy?" she adds and then peers up at me. Gauging my reaction.

The mention of his name ... It still affects me. I think it always will. Maddie has horrible timing, though.

"At first." I take a sip of coffee and try not to let the overthinking and insecurity rule this conversation. Baby steps. "It felt like I was cheating on him," I croak out, my chest feeling tight. "But that was in the beginning and it's been a few weeks now, so ..."

"Cheating?" Sue's reaction is complete with a huff. "Um no, that's what he did to you," Sue says with a firm voice that grabs my attention. She rests a hand on my forearm. "Moving on is *not* cheating ... But you know you two ..." she trails off then purses her lips with her eyes on me as if she doesn't know if she should say what's on her mind.

"Say it." My voice is strong as I speak. I just want to get it out there, like ripping off a bandage. Even if it hurts, I need to hear it. I didn't expect her next statement, though.

"I worry about you and Mason." It's like being thrown into ice water. I thought she had something to say about

Jace. She didn't really care for him. She didn't hide it either. I wasn't prepared for her to talk about Mason, though. "It doesn't have anything to do with Jace." She waves her hand through the air as if to thoroughly drive home that message and then continues. "You know I never liked Jace much, especially after he hurt you." *Cheating. After cheating on me.* That's what she means. We'd only ever been with each other, so he said he'd been curious and he swore it was a mistake. I forgave him. We moved past that together. Sue never did but it wasn't her marriage and it wasn't her decision.

"Why are you worried?" I ask cautiously, tapping my nails along the side of the cup and removing the thoughts of that infidelity from my mind. "It's nothing serious." I bite the inside of my cheek; even to me, that sounded like a lie.

"That right there," Sue says as she leans back and points her finger at me. "I worry that you don't know what casual dating is or how to act with a fuck buddy, or whatever this is for Mason."

If they could hear the way my heart protests, she'd be doubly worried.

I clear my throat and spit out my next words. "He said he could give me more so it's not exactly just for fun." The tips of my fingers tingle and then go numb as both Sue and Maddie stare at me for a moment. *Say something.*

"What?" Maddie interjects, scooting her stool closer to the table. Her pink dress is pulled tight across her breasts as she leans forward and says, "What did he mean by 'more?'" She's as giddy as a schoolgirl.

"Yeah, what the fuck did he mean by more?" Sue asks, her skepticism obvious. Even Kat looks up from her phone to listen. She's barely said a word since sitting down other than to apologize for having to work and that she swears she's listening. I suppose now she really is.

"I don't know. I just ..." I stop and focus on Sue, my former cheerleader and the one I know I need to convince. "I was worried too," I say, making sure I'm careful with my words, "and I told him that I didn't know if I could handle 'just sex' because I would probably want more, and he said he could give me that." I think back to that night just two weeks ago, or has it been more now? I'm fairly certain that's what I said and how he answered. "It makes me feel secure, that I can be open about how I'm feeling and that he's receptive to it."

Maddie lets out a small sigh of satisfaction, like a young girl in puppy love. She's the only one obviously happy about what I've said. Sue taps her nails rhythmically on the table and Kat hasn't moved, still watching me like a hawk. Like I'm prey and she's just circling in the skies above, waiting to strike.

"Can I just ask a question?" Kat says, setting down her phone and turning her full attention to me. "Why him? Are you sure you want more ... and with him?"

"Okay ... I didn't expect that as the follow-up question." It takes a moment for me to put my thoughts into words.

"Mason is nothing like the man I *should* be with. But that man is gone and I'm not interested in replacing him."

I take another sip of coffee, feeling defensive and like I'm not sure that I really want to even have this conversation.

"Are you wanting to settle down with him?" Kat asks and waits for me to look at her. "Like are you dating, dating?"

"I'm not settling down or replacing—" Jace's name gets caught in my throat.

"Oh no, oh no." Kat's quick to correct herself, reaching out for me even though my hands are now clasped in my lap. "I didn't mean ... I don't know what I mean."

"Maybe he's a rebound," Sue chimes in with a shrug and then looks up at the menu on the other side of the room. The text is fairly large, but she's not reading it. All four of us have that menu memorized. "It doesn't have to be serious," she says and the other two women all nod in agreement, but I'm certain it's to placate me.

"Yeah," I say noncommittally, holding up my coffee and looking back at Kat for her response. "What if he's just a rebound?"

Kat picks up her phone again but she doesn't look at it. She bites her lip and asks, "Can we meet him?"

"For fuck's sake, Kat," Sue says from across the table, practically glaring at her. "You don't introduce a rebound to your friends."

"Is that a rule?" Kat bites back. "He likes drinks, we like

drinks, let's all just have drinks."

"It's weird!" Sue's brow is comically raised as she stares back at Kat like she can't be serious. "Just let her do what she wants to do," she says and Sue's last sentence is hushed.

"I'd like to meet him," Maddie says with a sweet, innocent tone. Staring at each one of my friends in turn, I know they're all looking out for me. All nervous like I was weeks ago.

"I've got this," I say to all three of them at once. "It's just sex, but there's a level of respect and understanding." I nod my head. "That's what the *more* is."

A soft sigh leaves me and I feel like I've fixed my nonexistent problem. That's exactly what this is. "It's just a mutually beneficial arrangement with respect, and sex of course."

Both Kat and Sue are silent, each nodding and probably not convinced with my words. Each for their own reason, and I love them for their concern.

"I have a meeting with my CPA," I say as I glance down at my phone. I was going to walk there but there's no way in hell I'm going to make it on time now. "I have to go," I huff out as I reach down to grab my leather tote off the floor.

"Hey," Kat says. "You're happy?" she asks with all seriousness.

I stand up, slinging the purse over my shoulder and pushing the stool back. "Yeah," I say and that smile comes back. "I'm happy."

I expect some kind of guilt or feeling of inevitable doom,

but the girls all smile and Maddie squeals with delight. My chest feels empty, as if I'm lying to myself and afraid that someone will expose it. But I am happy. This is what happiness feels like, isn't it?

"That's what matters," Kat says with finality.

"Damn right," Sue says, adding her two cents as she grabs her purse to join me.

"Want to share a cab?" she asks, the conversation of Mason and whatever the hell I'm doing with him long gone. At least for now.

CHAPTER 21

JULIA

This office sucks. Even as a writer, there isn't a better word to describe it that comes to mind. For starters, it's always dark. Crossing my ankles and shifting in the chair, I don't understand why Mr. Allen Walker never opens the curtains. I used to joke with Kat that he's really a vampire. The plain white shades aren't thick but they're very good at blocking out what little sunlight would shine through the windows to my right. The office practically brushes against the neighboring building. Through the small gap where the fabric panels meet, I can see the old brick from Parks Towers next door. I'd rather look at that and have some sunlight than stare at closed curtains.

I scoot back on the chair with my purse in my lap, feeling more and more uncomfortable.

"Miss Summers." Allen addresses me as he always has since I was a little girl and even after I was married, but it feels different now. He shuts the door behind him, a smile on his face as he shoves his wire-rimmed glasses up the bridge of his nose. Fine lines and wrinkles crease around his eyes as he holds out a hand for me. I stand up, the lightweight chair scooting back on the thin carpet as I shake his hand.

"It's been too long," he says warmly. I nod my head and smile politely although I disagree.

The last time I was here was a few days after Jace passed away. That day, Allen made sure to call me by my legal name and not the name I grew up with. The memory makes the tiny hairs on the back of my neck stand on edge as I clear my throat and retake my seat. Uncomfortable as it may be, it's the only one I've got.

It seems he's forgotten that Summers still isn't my legal name. I look down at my barren hand and think that's my fault. I took my ring off months ago. That was easy, all things considered, but changing my name is something else entirely. It would be like erasing Jace, and I won't do that.

"It has," I say lightheartedly, pulling down my light gray pencil skirt and readjusting in my seat as he takes his on the other side of the desk.

My chair is small and uncomfortable, while his is large

and practically molds to his body.

I shake off the anxiety running through me as I straighten my back and ask, "What is it that you needed me to sign?"

A rough laugh fills the room as he shakes his head then says, "Not just yet. I need decisions, Miss Summers."

My body tenses at hearing my name but I bite my tongue. "Of course. What kind of decisions?"

"As acting advisor to your estate and investments, I need you to look these over," he says as he pulls out several folders and sets them in front of me. My brow furrows as I open the first and then the second. I don't know a thing about any of these. I've never been involved with investments and stocks.

"I—" I start to say and then let out an uneasy breath as I continue, "Is there a way that I could take your advisement, Mr. Walker?"

He turns his head to the side and raises his brow as if to say I should have done that a long time ago. "I advised your husband when he made these transactions. Unfortunately, the choices now are to stay and keep your money in a losing bet or to withdraw and lose a substantial amount."

My body goes cold as I take in his words. "I don't understand."

"Mr. Anderson was adamant about buying these properties and he assured me that it would be worth the risk, but I've waited over nine months now and there's still no growth since the drop."

"The drop?" I ask him, feeling the blood drain from my face. Jace never mentioned buying any properties. "This was with our personal assets? Not the business?"

He nods at my question, taking in a deep inhale. "They were on the decline when he purchased them. He was a bit surprised that they continued to drop, yes." Mr. Walker leans back, waiting for my reaction.

"How much of a decline?"

"Fourteen million."

I close my eyes, gripping the edge of the seat for a moment. Fourteen million. That's ... I can barely think straight. When we married, I know my assets were around twenty million. How could he take such a large chunk and not disclose any of this to me?

"There's still nearly six million invested so you can withdraw if you'd like. I like to say you've never lost money until you sell, but the fact is that I still believe you're not going to see the return your deceased husband was banking on."

My entire body is tense and on edge. Fourteen fucking million dollars. Fourteen million! I want to scream and curse, I want to throw up. It takes me a moment to gather myself to be able to respond.

"Why am I just learning about this now?" I ask him in a voice that's more filled with anger than full of shock and grief. I flip through a few pages with shaking hands, reading through them, but not actually reading a word.

Fourteen million and now I can only sell for six? I'm going to be sick.

"Well, it was stable but it's recently gone up just a touch, and I'm of the opinion that you should take advantage of the current climate."

My mouth hangs open just a bit as I look back at Mr. Walker, eyeing his blue suit and thin red tie. I blink a few times, then fall back into my chair and shut the folder.

"Is this all of the investments?" I ask, realizing how little I knew of Jace's dealings. For the first time in my life, I'm worried. I've never had to concern myself with income. I've been blessed and grateful, but I wasn't careless. This right here, this feels like careless to a maximum degree and I'm embarrassed. I'm sick to my stomach and mortified.

I swallow thickly and cross my legs, not able to stop my foot from rocking back and forth in the air. It's only as I sit here, my mouth feeling dry and my body like ice, that I realize I know nothing about my current financial situation. I trusted Jace to handle all this.

"Allen," I say as I pick at the clutch in my lap and look up at the man I grew up with. He's an old friend of my father and I do trust him, but right now I feel unsettled.

"Yes, Julia?" he asks.

"Financially speaking," I say then pause, taking in a steadying breath before I continue, "is everything all right?"

He takes a moment to answer me and the time ticks by

slowly while I wait for his reply.

He opens his mouth, looking down at the desk but doesn't say a word and dread hits me. "You're going to be fine, Miss Summers. You will be." He puts strength behind his words and looks straight into my eyes as he speaks.

I should be relieved, but he didn't exactly answer my question.

"It's going to be difficult getting this money back, especially considering the amount of debt you went into when remodeling your home."

"What?" I feel struck by his last statement. "We didn't go into debt." I got everything I wanted on that remodel because it was funded by the money I'd made with my first publishing contract. It was my personal reward to myself. "I know how every penny was spent and I know it was paid for with the money I brought in."

I can't help that my voice is full of panic and my tone is accusatory. I sit there on the edge of my seat, waiting for a response from Allen. I swallow the lump in my throat as he clicks on his mouse and takes off his glasses, scrolling through a row of spreadsheets.

"The remodel put you in quite a bit of debt, I'm sorry to say." I shake my head in disbelief as he adds, "If you were to sell the apartment, it could potentially make its money back."

Chills travel down every inch of my body as I take one breath, then two. "What apartment?" I ask him, my voice deathly low.

"The one downtown on Pacific Street. The one that was remodeled this past year."

My world spins on its axis and I grip the arms of the chair. "Mr. Walker? I don't own an apartment on Pacific." I lick my dry lips, my body coiled, my muscles feeling tense and tight.

There's a pause, filled with more ticks of the clock. "Well, your husband did and that was left to you. As was everything else in his will. So you do own an apartment on Pacific."

"Why wasn't I told about this sooner?" I ask, focusing my attention on something other than the fact that my husband bought and remodeled an apartment without me knowing. Betrayal consumes me but oddly, I feel numb to it. As if I'd known all along. As if I'd turned a blind eye. It's not naivety or trustworthiness. It's me being stupid. All the late nights at the office, all the weekend trips ... My skin pricks and a numbing tingle goes through me. He told me it was just once when I found him in bed with another woman. I try to breathe in easier, but my throat is closing.

Disbelief is outrageous. He didn't. He wasn't cheating on me. There's no way.

"You were given the paperwork, Julia. You signed everything after the funeral."

I look up at Allen, feeling betrayed by him just as much as my husband. I want to question him, scream at him. But at the same time, I don't care. I had this coming to me.

I didn't know about this debt. I didn't know about the

apartment. I didn't know about a damn thing because I trusted them.

"I was mourning," I say and I can barely get out the words. They're cold and stagnant. Just a lame excuse for my ignorance.

"I'm sorry, Mrs. Anderson." He starts to say something else but I rise from my chair, a bitter taste in my mouth as I bite out, "Don't call me that."

He cocks a brow at me as I start to leave. "You need to sign these, Julia," he says matter-of-factly, speaking to me like my father does. Ignoring my emotions and simply telling me what I need to do.

My shoulders shudder as I open the door with my back to him and grip the cold brass knob for dear life.

"Email them to me," I tell him. "Email *everything* to me."

"I suggest you read them quickly," he says to my back as I walk through the door.

I nod my head but I don't verbally respond; I don't trust myself to speak. I don't look back at him and I don't even breathe until I'm in the elevator. I can't relax though, even in the empty, closed-off space. I want to sag against the wall, gripping the steel handles. I want to hit the emergency button and give in to the pathetic emotions of sadness and betrayal.

More than any of that, I want to see this apartment and I want to see how the hell my money was spent. I need to get myself together and figure out how deep of a hole I'm in and more importantly, how to get out.

CHAPTER 22

MASON

Knock. *Knock. Knock.* My knuckles rap against Jules's door quickly. A second passes and I take a look around, shoving my hands into my suit pockets. The Upper East Side screams old money and is far more traditional compared to downtown where I live.

My father's home is only a few blocks from here.

Jules's street is different from where I grew up, though. The cream stone and intricate carvings have history to them. Real history. I glance back at the small iron picket fence and gate in front of her house. The city sidewalk is just beyond it, littered with people walking by.

I rock on my heels and knock again, wondering what they

think of this house.

It looks like wealth and with the well-maintained garden, it only adds to the beauty of the old house.

I've been inside Julia's home a handful of times now, and it's odd that I feel nervous about being here now. It's because I'm coming through the front door in daylight. I smirk at the thought, but it's true. My forehead pinches as I knock again, using the large iron door knocker this time.

The door swings open and there's my Jules, but she doesn't stay there long. She leaves the door hanging open and disappears inside, claiming that she has to get something, but I didn't hear what.

"Jules?" I call out after her, placing a hand on the heavy red door and peeking inside after her. The door creaks and I second-guess going inside after her, but she doesn't answer me.

Taking a few steps inside, I flick on the light switch to my right before shutting the front door. A large crystal chandelier lights up the large hallway. The ceilings are taller than they seem at night. Paisley wallpaper in shades of pale blue and cream covers the upper half of the walls with a deeper blue painted below the chair rail.

It's modern and updated with a feminine and elegant touch, definitely not my taste, but it still holds the classic beauty of the home. A mix of modern and traditional. It's all Jules.

"Jules," I call out again, pocketing my keys and wiping my shoes on the mat before stepping onto the plush area rug in the foyer.

"I'm sorry," I hear Jules say through the hall before I see her. She rounds the corner of what looks like the dining room, both hands on her left ear as she slips an earring into place. She's barefoot, wearing a navy blue dress with white polka dots and a skinny white leather belt at her waist. She's gorgeous as always, but something's off. Something's wrong although I can't tell what.

"Everything okay?" I ask carefully, staying right where I am as she bends down to slip on a pair of navy blue heels.

"Fine, just fine." She shakes out her hair and stands upright, taking a step toward me before turning on her heel and heading back the way she came.

I follow her into the dark dining room. It doesn't look a damn thing like a dining room, though. The furniture is all here, but stacks of papers cover the table, along with a laptop. On top of the buffet is a printer. She's using the room as an office.

"Sorry about the mess." Her voice is dampened as she turns around. "I just need my purse." She starts to walk past me, making her way to the door, but I put my arm out, my palm against the doorway and wait for her to look at me.

When she does, my heart drops. Her eyes are rimmed in red. Although her makeup is flawless, she can't hide that she was crying. Not from me.

"What's wrong?" It comes out as a question, but it's more of a command.

Her lips are the same dark red shade they were when I first met her and as she parts them, my eyes are drawn to them. She doesn't say anything though, she merely licks them and turns away from me. For the first time since we met, she's deliberately disobeying me. Hiding from me.

"I don't want to talk about it." She pushes my arm away, to leave me and deny me again, but I'm not letting this go. I grip her hip tight enough that she stops and looks at me.

"That's not how this works. I told you, if you're with me, you're with me." Her hard expression vanishes as I speak to her, replaced by nothing but hurt.

"You don't own me." She bites out the words meant to make me mad, meant to destroy the ease between us.

"It's not about that, Jules." My voice is low as I release her. She doesn't walk off; she stands there waiting for my next move. She has to know how good this is between us. She knows whatever the hell it is, I'll take the burden from her.

"I don't like seeing you upset." I bring my lips closer to hers. "Tell me what's wrong, so I can fix it." I open my mouth to give her a reason not to push me away, to tell her that she can trust me. That I care for her, to tell her everything I know she wants to hear, but I can't bring myself to do it. Luckily, I don't have to.

She moves her hands to her face for only a moment, her expression crumpling before she falls into my chest. She gives in to me so easily. It's addictive. I wrap my arms around her, feeling her shoulders shake and shudder with a soft sob.

"I didn't want to cry again," she says into my chest, muffled by the suit jacket and her hands still covering her face. She inhales deeply as I bend down, running my hand up and down her back in soothing strokes and kiss her hair repeatedly.

"It's all right, whatever it is, I'll take care of it." I don't know why I promise her something I know I may not be able to accommodate. It's stupid of me to say it and it gets the reaction it should from an independent woman like Jules. She pushes away from me, wiping under her eyes and taking a shuddering breath.

"It's nothing you—" she stops to close her eyes and calm herself. "It can't be fixed." She glances at a photograph in a silver frame behind her on the wall and then wipes under her eyes again, walking to a large mirror on the far side of the dining room.

I only catch a glimpse of the photograph before turning my back to it. It's from her wedding day and he's in it. Obviously. He was her husband after all.

Panic races through me and a sick feeling churns my stomach. "It's about your husband?"

She peeks over her shoulder, looking guilty. The fucking irony. "I'm sorry."

"Don't be." My steps are just as careful as my words as I walk over to her, placing a hand on her delicate shoulder and watching her in the mirror. "Is everything okay?"

"No," she answers quickly and sniffles once. She's already

fixed her makeup and looking as though she's back to pretending nothing's wrong, but then her eyes meet mine in the mirror. Her baby blues are filled with anger and an unforgiving chill. "He had an apartment," she says with certainty. "A place for his mistresses or one-night stands or whatever they were."

I attempt a look that expresses shock, but none of that is news to me. I wasn't sure if she knew. For the first time since meeting her, I feel guilty for not telling her. As if somehow I could have saved her this heartache if I'd given her a piece of the truth. Only a piece.

She laughs something wicked and sad, a mix of both as she shakes her head and says, "You think I'm pathetic, don't you? A housewife who had no idea what her husband was doing behind her back." Her voice is strained toward the end of the statement and the strength leaves her with each word. I hate how she does this. How she blames herself, belittles herself. She's stronger than she knows. And worth so much more.

"What he did is a reflection of himself, not you." Taking another step closer to her, I stand behind her with her back touching my chest, just barely. "You aren't pathetic, Jules." I kiss the side of her neck, my eyes on hers in the mirror as I say, "I'd never think that."

"I do," she says. "He cheated once. He was so upset. He cried and swore up and down he'd never do it again. And I believed him."

My heart beats erratically and I'm desperate to ask who

he cheated with. To see if Jules knows her name. I keep my mouth closed and wait for more from her.

"I believed him." The pain comes through in her words as she turns in my arms, placing her small hands on the lapels of my jacket. Her eyes travel along the buttons of my shirt, her fingers soon following. "I really thought he was good to me."

I pull away slightly, taking her wrists gently in my hands and getting her attention. "I'm sorry," I tell her with true sympathy but it comes out rough and short, shocking her.

She pulls away from me. "I am too," she says to the ground, turning around and brushing the hair out of her face. "I think maybe tonight—"

I can hear the excuse already, I can see her pushing me away and I'm not going to let it happen. There's no way I'm leaving until I know she's still mine.

Each time she questions me or what's going on between us, I feel the need to hold her tighter.

"Come here," I command her. She stops in her tracks, peeking up at me through thick lashes with a question in her eyes. She doesn't ask whatever it is though, she obeys me, taking two small steps back to me in those heels.

"He was a fool to cheat on you." As I speak, I brush my thumb along her delicate jaw.

She huffs a small laugh at me and I didn't expect that. I narrow my eyes as she says, "You're a well-known player, Mason." The humor vanishes and her smile fades to nothing as she adds, "You don't have to pretend to care. I'll be fine."

My chest tightens with anger. She can have an attitude about him all she wants. But there are boundaries when it comes to us. I won't allow her to demean our relationship. "Bend over the table." I grit the words out between my teeth. I don't even think twice about it.

She merely blinks at me, shocked. She should have known better.

"Now, Jules." My voice comes out hard and I almost take it back. But this is the man I am and this is what she's going to get. There's a war brewing between us, causing the air to suffocate me. I need Jules for the woman she truly is, not this version that the memory of her husband brought back.

She holds my gaze for a moment and my pulse flickers, thinking I'm going to lose her, but she caves before I even blink, submitting just like she wants to. *Good girl.*

She presses her hips against the table, slowly leaning down to lay her upper body against the tabletop. That's the beauty of our relationship—she wants to give in. She desperately wants to trust someone and not be hurt.

"Lift up your dress."

I hear her breathing pick up. "Mason—" she starts to say.

"No, no talking. No excuses." I palm my dick but I have no intention of fucking her. This is all about pleasing her and showing her what she means to me. Showing her what I can give her. "Lift up your dress and show me your pussy." I crouch down behind her as she slowly pulls the cotton fabric up her thighs and exposes her black panties.

My fingers trail up her thighs slowly to her ass, then up to the small of her back, pressing her down flat. I carefully push the panties out of my way, taking a languid lick of her pussy. My tongue brushes along the lacy material and I almost rip them as I pull them farther away, but decide to put my fingers to better use.

I play at her clit first, gently running my nail across the swollen nub and then back to her entrance. Goosebumps travel along her body. It doesn't take long before she's glistening for me, her wet folds begging for my attention.

She hums as she relaxes on the table. It's going to be a slow build for her. I don't care about our dinner reservations. She'll have to deal with being late.

I slide my middle finger deep inside her as I stand up behind her, keeping my other hand on her hip. Her eyes are closed as I fuck my finger in and out of her, loosening her up and testing her readiness. Remembering my anger, I pick up my pace and slip another finger into her.

"Come on, Jules," I say and kiss the back of her neck. "Tell me again how I don't care." A strangled cry leaves her as I press against her clit and she whimpers an apology, still struggling to get away from the intense pleasure.

I push three fingers deep inside of her tight pussy, stroking against her front wall right where that sensitive bundle of nerves is and I don't let up as she moans. Her body writhes in an attempt to get away, pulling at the tablecloth and kicking one leg out, but I've got her pinned down to the table with my hip. One hand continues to rub her hard nub ruthlessly, while the other is inside of her dripping wet cunt.

"I would never cheat on you." And then I tell her, "I'd never take advantage of you." She has no idea how true those words are.

"Mason." She cries out my name as she tightens around my fingers. *My. Name.* I want her to come undone screaming my name. To find her release with what I do to her all because she let me. All she has to do is give in to me.

"Tell me you understand, Jules." I'm not letting her get off until I hear her say it. I swear to God I'll stop it all if she doesn't give me that.

I may be holding back the truth, but I'm not lying.

"Yes," she moans out as she thrashes her head.

"Yes what?"

"Yes, Mason."

I smile into her hair, slowing my pace and making her whimper as she desperately rocks her pussy into my hand.

"Yes, Mason what?"

My heart thrums in my chest, but I need to hear her say it. I don't want that shit with her husband having anything to do with what we have with each other.

"You wouldn't do that." She bites her lip looking back at

me with a plea for mercy. "You wouldn't hurt me."

I crash my lips into hers and fuck her cunt with my fingers, relentlessly pressing against her swollen nub. She cries into my mouth as her release hits her hard, her head banging on the table as she tries to pull away from the intensity. I don't let up, coaxing out every single bit of her orgasm from her.

Her back bows with tremors still rocking through her. This is how I want her, always.

No worries in her soft blue eyes, only a look of pleasure on her face.

A look that I put there.

My dick's hard as a fucking rock, but this isn't for me. She looks over her shoulder, still panting with her fingers gripping the cream tablecloth. She's waiting for me to take from her. To fuck her right here and now. But that picture of her husband is right there.

Part of me wants to do it. To force that beautiful cunt to spasm on my dick in front of him. To show him how a real man would treat her. But I can't. I need to get the fuck out of here.

I pull her hips back, her ass pressed against my hard cock.

Her lashes flutter and her wide eyes look back at me, waiting for whatever I have to say. "Dinner first, sweetheart." I kiss her gently then brush her clit through her panties and smile as a tremor runs through her body and forces her head back against my shoulder.

I kiss the dip in her neck and whisper in her ear, "Tonight."

CHAPTER 23

JULIA

Naive and stupid, this shit has to end.
What did I think? I can't comprehend.
Mistakes belong where they're made, in the past.
I knew better, I knew this wouldn't last.
It left me numb, dead in the ditch.
Love is wrong and my heart's a bitch.

I stare out the window of Mason's car as the city lights flicker on, although it's not even dark yet. Classical music fills the cabin and my body is still humming from the rush of pleasure he gave me moments ago.

But nothing is okay.

I need to end this. What's the saying? Get over one man by getting under another? I'm not interested for two reasons:

I'm not over what Jace did to me.

I'm not ready for another man to do the same.

That's what I've been telling myself all day ever since I left Mr. Walker's office. I don't have time for fooling around and I'm not ready for anything serious. And that's what this has become; it's staring me right in the eyes.

This is serious. It's too serious. I'm suffocating and what's worse is that the minute I'm with Mason, the very second that he looks at me just right, says all the right things, the moment his lips press against mine and his skin touches mine, I'm done for.

I'm head over heels for Mason. I didn't even hesitate when he told me to bend over my dining room table for him. I didn't hesitate in the parking garage either. He's had me from the very night we met.

There's something about him that makes me weak, and I'm so very tired of being weak.

I can't do this. I need to end it. Just the very thought ... it hurts.

"I—" I start to give him the honest truth, my whole truth. I don't know how to be okay on my own and that's my priority right now. That's the bottom line. Pressing my back against the smooth leather and glancing at him in the driver's seat, the words are right there on the tip of my tongue. *I can't do this anymore.* I don't know what's real and where I stand with anything, and I need space to figure it all out, but my phone goes off in my purse, the ringtone loud and obnoxious.

I let out a frustrated sigh, pulling it out and just missing a call from my mother. I almost call her back, but then I see the text messages. Dozens of them.

I hit the first one from Kat.

The last message makes me sick to my stomach. *It's going to be okay.*

What's going to be okay? What now? I scroll up to read the messages starting from the top.

OMG I just saw, are you okay?

Minutes later:

I can't believe he did that to you!

Everything is all right, we're going to get it taken down.

A chill slips like ice down my skin.

I don't have to ask her what she's talking about. Maddie sent me a link to the online article. It's already been taken down, but she screenshotted it.

My heart sinks as I skim it, but my eyes keep flickering to the picture. It shows me and Jace, and right next to it, Jace and some beautiful woman. It's obvious what the article was about and it makes me sick. My throat goes dry and tears prick my eyes.

Really? They posted this now? I think back to who I told and who would have heard about the apartment. It's up for sale as of 4:00 p.m. today, so that was only five hours for someone to dig up the dirt. I can barely breathe.

"Jules?" Mason's voice doesn't stop me from reading. It's

not the worst thing that's been said about me but it's not kind, and it's not true. I wasn't turning a blind eye. There's a difference. I truly didn't know.

My anger only increases when I see what they're saying about me now. I'm not running around town. I'm not spreading my legs ... I can't even finish this article. The last paragraph I read is:

Now that her husband is gone, she's letting loose but choosing the same kind of man. The socialite doesn't seem to care about her reputation anymore.

Whoever gave the details to the *Daily Word* knows that I'm seeing Mason but they don't know how often, since they claim he cheated on me two nights ago. I've been with him every single night for weeks now.

Every insecurity in me is replaced by raw rage.

Heat dances along my skin. I'm not this person that they're painting me to be. I'm on the edge of breaking into a million pieces. I told Mason this is why I didn't want us to be public. I knew something like this would happen. *I knew it!*

Is that a stage of grief? Wanting to murder everyone?

I just want to be left alone.

I bite the inside of my cheek and place the phone in my lap as Mason's hand lands on my thigh.

"What's wrong?" he asks, his eyes darting from me to

the road.

"Take me home," I say. I don't bother to answer his question and I lick my dry lips. My heart hurts too much.

"What's wrong?" This time his voice is harder. The one he uses right before he turns me into a damn rag doll for his will and then magically fixes everything.

I'm done listening to men and I'm done rolling over for them.

"What's wrong is that this isn't working for me anymore," I finally tell him, although I don't know how, in an even tone that splits my heart right down the center. Guilt consumes the anger immediately. It slices through every emotion with the sharpest knife, the cut clean and quick, but the blood is pouring out and I know it's not going to stop anytime soon.

I lean my head back against the headrest. "I want to go home."

Mason's quiet although his pissed-off expression reads loud and clear as he pushes down his turn signal.

The silence stretches between us and this awkward, horrific dread makes me squirm. I find myself going back to the screenshots. What's really and truly messed up is that I feel safe and happy with Mason. If it were a different time, I could easily fall for him. I *am* easily falling for him. It's as if I'm tumbling down a well in slow motion, giving me enough time as I fall to look up and admire the stonework before crashing to the black bottom of the abyss.

"I can't do this anymore," I say, reaffirming myself and

him. "I need to be on my own."

He doesn't look at me and a long moment passes before he says anything at all. Mason's voice is low when he asks, "Because of an article?" He grips the leather steering wheel until his knuckles are white. "I'll take care of it," he says. I'm sure he could fix all my problems. He's so good at that.

But I need to fix myself. I need to be whole before I can give myself so completely to someone.

"It's not the article." The words drop one by one and my eyes burn.

"Is it your prick of a former husband?" he asks with disgust so apparent, I hate him in this moment. I confided in him about my deceased husband and yes, he may have hurt me, cheated on me and lied to me, but that's not for Mason to judge. I still don't even know how to feel about it all. How dare he speak about him like that?

"That's exactly why this needs to stop." My heart rages in my chest, hating me for being so raw, but I can't stop.

"I'm not okay," I say, feeling a burn in my eyes dampened from tears, but I don't care, let them fall. Let everyone see and call me whatever they want. "I haven't been okay and I've been running from it. You can't just fix me. I can't fall into another man's arms and forget about everything I'm going through."

With shaking hands, I almost throw my phone when it pings again. The absurdity of my entire world crashing down around me feels too overwhelming. I'm too hot, too angry, too miserable.

"I just want to go home." There's a finality in the statement and it feels like razors at the back of my throat.

"Stop," Mason commands me as he slows down at a crosswalk. "Just take it easy." His entire demeanor changes to something placating, as if he's talking to a wounded animal. It only makes me angrier.

"No, I won't stop. What do you want from me, Mason?"

A part of me is hoping he really is my knight in shining armor. Part of me wants to be weak. I want him to solve all my problems and just crawl into his bed every night, moving on to a new life and leaving the old one in shattered pieces behind me.

I know it's wrong. It's giving in and denying my responsibilities. But God, I want it. My heart is suffocating, hoping for him to say just the right things to convince me to be his, to forget everything else. Just like he has from the first night I met him. "What is it that you want from me?" My voice shakes.

"Jules." He says my name and looks at me with a gaze I don't understand.

"Just tell me right now, what do you want?" I swallow the spikes growing in my throat, but they don't move. They only grow larger and sharper and make the words scrape as they leave me. "I can't give myself to you right now unless—"

"Unless what?" Mason asks so quickly he cuts me off. His

reaction makes the pain that much deeper because I don't have an answer.

I can't give myself to him unless this is forever. Unless I can trust him but right now I can't trust anyone. The harsh reality is what truly does me in. I don't trust anyone anymore. I don't want to love anyone anymore.

I can't breathe as I take off my seat belt. My townhome is only a few blocks away. My shelter. My sanctuary and my grave. My hands shake as the seat belt pulls back, hissing and hating me just as much as I hate myself.

"I can't," I say. "I'm sorry," I whisper.

I unlock the door and push it open. A car drives by close, but I shut the door quickly, avoiding Mason's reach for me. His fingers brush against my back as I get out.

"Jules!" Mason calls after me. I cross the lane, the other driver beeping and holding down his horn. Go ahead, hate me too.

The sound of a door opening alerts me to the fact that Mason is out of his car, leaving it parked in the middle of the road and already holding up traffic. "Jules!" he screams but I keep running. The horns don't stop and it's not lost on me that what I did was wrong.

I rush past the onlookers and ignore the dirty looks and stares. My shoulders rise with a heavy breath. I need to go home. Tears stream down my face. I need to take care of myself and figure out what the hell I'm doing with my life.

Tires screech and make my head throb as Mason drives alongside me now, slow and causing more traffic to build up.

I ignore Mason as I whip open the iron gate. I don't stop until I'm safe inside my house, my back to the hard door, my body shaking and my heart hammering.

I hate myself for running from Mason.

But this is a reckless distraction.

I cover my mouth as another sob leaves me, slowly falling to my knees on the floor.

He's a good man and he deserves someone better than me.

Someone who doesn't have all these problems.

Someone who can fall for him freely and be with him openly.

I sag against the door, letting it all out, still hoping he'll come bang on the door and plead with me to explain. I can't be this person, though. It's better that he doesn't.

It's the way we both knew it would end. I envisioned it would be him leaving me though, not the other way around. I take a shuddering breath, feeling exactly how I should, like shit. Not that any of it matters.

It was never meant to be. That's all there is to it.

CHAPTER 24

MASON

Seventeen. I called her seventeen fucking times. It hurts worse knowing she left me for something other than the one reason she should. Knowing that I couldn't keep her on my own. I held on too tight. It's my own fucking mistake.

But I saw what I could do for her.

What I could do *to* her.

And that made me feel ... something other than this. This fucking hate that I have brewing inside of me.

What the hell did I expect? I expected to keep her. For her to learn to love me. For that to cancel out what I'd done.

The ice clinks in my glass as I grab a bottle of Macallan single malt.

No reasoning or any amount of logic justifies why I feel betrayed and alone. Not a damn explanation can leave me feeling as though this is something that doesn't need to be mended. The liquor sloshes in the bottle as I read the label, my fingers playing with the seal.

My father gave me this bottle as a gift when I started the company with Liam. When I told him I was going into business for myself, but still doing what I loved. I felt so much pride that day. My breathing quickens and my grip on the bottle tightens.

Relax. I grit my teeth, feeling an uneasy tightness settle through my body.

Jules was a sweet distraction; how fucking ironic. She pulled me away from reality. She made me feel like I had time. Like I had a choice.

I toss the seal onto my sideboard buffet, opening the bottle and not bothering to appreciate the rich scent before pouring it into the glass.

If my father were here, he'd give me hell for drinking it over ice.

"But that bastard's not here," I sneer under my breath. "No one is." The last thought leaves my chest feeling hollow. I take a long drink of the whisky that flows so easily. Burning and traveling through my chest, down deeper and stirring in the pit of my stomach. My head still tipped back I take another and finish the damn thing, the ice frigid against my lips. I slam the glass down a little harder than I should and let the liquor hit me.

It takes too long and I find myself gazing straight ahead to the family portrait sitting on top of the buffet. This room, the dining room, is the only room in the whole place where there's a picture of anyone.

The rest of the house is devoid of anything truly personal. But what do I really have that's personal anyway? My lacrosse stick and all those fucking uniforms stayed at my parents' where they belonged. I'm sure they were thrown away long ago.

I pour more of the whisky into the glass, feeling my breathing slow as my body sways and I remember the first day I walked in here.

I'd just gotten all new clothes, all new furniture, all new everything. This home was the start of the professional version of me. All that was in the cardboard box I was holding were a handful of old tee shirts and a few postcards from a friend of mine in Germany I'd met after I graduated high school and got my first job in construction. We've lost touch since then.

I take a sip, listening to the ice rattle against the glass. The whisky sits on my tongue and I press it against my teeth before swallowing. All the awards I've won are in my office. Framed and arranged just so on the wall.

My gaze drifts back to the portrait of the three of us. I'm standing between the two of them in it. I don't look a damn thing like her, like my mother. I'm the spitting image of my father. Mom's smile is soft, but her eyes are what sparkle. She was so expressive. Soft spoken, but she made what she said count.

She could make an entire room laugh by only speaking once the whole night. I let out a breath, looking at the firm hand my father has on my shoulder in the photograph.

He liked that about her. He told me once she was the perfect example of what a wife should be. That was before he caught her cheating.

I wonder if that man, the one she risked her marriage to sleep with, loved to hear her talk. I wonder if that's why she did it. Because she had more to say than just a single sentence.

I down the whisky, dragging out the chair at the head of the table and taking a seat. I sag and let my head lean back against the crest rail of the antique chair.

This room is so dark. With black textured wallpaper on the longest wall and the other three painted a soft gray, I wanted it to feel masculine. I remember telling the designer that. I told her I wanted it to feel like me.

On the right, centered in the room and next to the dark mahogany buffet, is a long gas fireplace. It's surrounded by a sleek marble hearth. More black. Even the light fixture in the room, a circular pendulum that holds the light inside, is black.

I huff a breath into the short glass and suck an ice cube into my mouth.

This is me.

A heart of fire that's never lit. A dark past that only holds a single moment of time in significance.

I wonder if that bitch designer knew what she was doing.

I kick the leg of the antique chair next to me. It's carved wood that's been stained. The deep brown leather of the chairs has a worn look to it.

What's ironic is how much I loved this room. I loved everything about it when I first laid eyes on it. The only addition I made was that fucking silver picture frame and then I filled that buffet with liquor.

Thank fuck I did that. I raise my glass even though it's empty, save for ice. "To you, you fucking prick," I toast the picture and take another ice cube into my mouth.

I crunch down, wondering if the last three words were for my father or for me.

Pushing the glass across the slick table that I've never sat at for more than a drink or two, I pull out my cell phone from my back pocket.

I fucking want Jules.

She's pure and sweet. Even if she overthinks every last detail, there's so much about her that I want to keep. I really shouldn't have her. I've already been given more than I deserve.

I can't do this anymore.

The screen lights up as I hear her words in my head. She shouldn't get to decide when it's over. Not by herself and not like that. Not because of something so fucking unimportant.

We work together. We make each other happy. I'm tired of living this life with nothing to fight for. I want her back.

My phone rings in my hand, startling me and I drop it on the table. It vibrates, moving slightly as the ringtone goes off again.

Groaning and rubbing my eyes, I feel the heat of the drunken night start to take me in before answering the call.

"Hello?" I think my voice is even. I'm fairly certain it comes out strong.

"Mason, we need to talk." I recognize Liam's voice immediately.

I brace my elbow on the table and rest my head in my hand before pinching the bridge of my nose. We do need to talk; we need to have a long talk about how I can't go through with this.

All the money is spent.

But I can't keep pushing forward.

I need to return it all to my father and cut ties. I need to turn him in.

Every bit of breath in my lungs leaves me, making my body feel light and my stomach sick. We're going to go fucking bankrupt, but I can't be under his thumb any longer.

"We need that investment from your father's firm." A sad, pathetic laugh leaves me as I register what Liam's said.

"We already have it." I stagger to the buffet, placing the phone on speaker, leaving it on the dining room table as I pour another glass. The bottle's already halfway gone. "We've already spent it," I say loud and clear as I bring the amber liquor to my lips.

This time I inhale the sweet scent. Fuck, it smells as good as it tastes.

"We need more." I gulp down the drink, staring at the phone on the table as Liam continues. "We got the estates on the Upper East Side and the committee approved the demolition plans."

As I take a step forward, I start to regret having the last two drinks. My head feels groggy and my body hot. "No, they didn't."

"I got it overturned. We've got everything approved, Mason." I can hear the glee in Liam's voice. Pride even. He claps on the other end of the phone, a rough laugh filling the room as it spins around me. "We just need that last check from your father."

Setting both of my elbows on the table to steady myself, I tell him, "We don't need shit from him."

It takes a moment for Liam to respond, "What?" He took so long I almost forgot he was on the phone.

"Are you drunk?" Liam asks, his annoyance only thinly veiled.

"No." I'm quick to deny it, but I know I am.

"What the hell's wrong with you?" he asks. "What's going on between the two of you?"

I shake my head, not wanting to answer. "We aren't taking shit from my father." It's all I can say.

"We are. We need those funds by Monday." Liam's voice is hard but also panicked.

"We'll find someone else." My eyes narrow as I steady my breathing and steel my resolve. I refuse to owe a man like him. I refuse to play by his rules.

"By Monday?" he says, raising his voice and the disbelief rings through. "Mason, we can't. We'll lose the deal. It's not like no one else was waiting for this property. It took almost a year to get it."

Liam's voice drones on as he lists off every reason why this plan is fucked. How we'll be ruined. How everything will fall around us.

I already knew it, though.

I stand, leaving the glass where it is and the bottle of whisky open, taking the phone and leaving the dining room.

"I don't give a fuck." I take a deep breath, listening to the silence on the other end of the phone. "I'm not taking another cent from him."

I have to face reality. Even if it fucking kills me.

CHAPTER 25

JULIA

Nothing is suffocating.
It cuts off the air.
Nothing is drowning,
But nothing is fair.
Nothing to hold and nothing to thrill.
When left with nothing, nothing can kill.

The air is crisp on the iron balcony. The thick canopy of oak trees just barely blocks the sounds of the city traffic. I've always loved the colors of autumn and the way the dark green leaves thin out and shift to gorgeous reds and burnt oranges.

They'll fall and wither away to nothing. Yet every spring they come back, good as new.

I've always loved their majestic natural beauty in the

middle of this concrete jungle. Not today, though.

It's not fair that they come back untarnished. It's not right that life continues after death ... only for those deserving.

Bundled in my favorite cashmere throw and sipping tea, I let out a deep breath, calming myself. I twist the cap to my flask and pour a bit of tincture into my tea. A small, faint chuckle leaves me as the liquid mixes with the now lukewarm tea. *Tincture.* Really, it's just vodka.

It used to be a tincture. It used to be just enough to take the pain away.

But sips turned to bottles as I preferred to feel numb.

Today is one of those days.

If I can roll out of bed and have the strength to tuck the sheets in and fluff the pillows, the day will be okay. That's what I'd tell myself over and over again when Jace first died. Sometimes it's true. All you need to do is make your bed and somehow the day is possible. As if simply pulling the sheets tight and smoothing out all the wrinkles is enough to hide the past and put the daily routine into motion.

Some days, it's all a lie.

All the time I spent with Mason ... all that time feels like a lie. Some fantasy I forced to convince myself that life could be okay again. That it could somehow mend itself.

I take a sip of the tea, but it only makes my throat feel more parched. Instead of gulping it down like I've been doing, it finds its place on the saucer and I press my palms against my sore eyes.

It's been so long since I've felt this empty. Since my heart has felt as though it's been torn open.

It doesn't make sense in the least. I was over him. I was making progress. True progress in healing by being okay with Jace being gone.

I was okay.

For the first time since his death, I felt like I had a reason to be happy. More importantly, like it was okay to be happy.

Glancing over my shoulder, I rub my tired eyes with the sleeve of my silk blouse. I thought I heard someone. Just for a second, I thought I heard someone behind me.

My first thought is Mason. That he's come back and he isn't taking no for an answer. I roll my eyes feeling my heart squeeze violently in my chest.

I can't make that situation more than what it was. A hookup, a fuck buddy, I don't have a clue. I know what it is now, though. It's over.

Settling back down in the iron chair, I snatch up my notepad. I haven't written like this in so long, but there are scribbles everywhere. It's all loose poetry, lazy I suppose. It tells the story of how Jace and I met when we were young. How we fit so well together and everyone told us we were meant to be.

My eyes close as I remember the day we first got together. I can still hear how the school bells went off as we walked on the sidewalk to get to class. I brushed my knuckles against his, waiting and hoping. It had to have been obvious to him. Maybe I was the one to make the first move, but he chose me. He threaded his fingers through mine and he didn't let go. He was a good man, not a perfect man. He was good to me. Or so I thought.

"I hate this." I utter the words beneath my breath and it comes out shaky. They say when someone dies, you remember the good times more than the bad. Rose-colored glasses or something like that. I have to keep reminding myself that there were bad times too. With all these articles, I'm not having a difficult time remembering.

There's guilt too, which is something that I don't want. I don't want to be angry at someone who will never again have the chance to defend himself.

How can I move forward when I'm too busy hating everything as I scribble down scenes of our fights in this notepad? I let the words flow and pour out all of it, but mostly his infidelity.

Creak. The creak of the floorboards behind me sends chills sweeping down my body. I stand abruptly from the chair and the iron scrapes on the balcony.

Every emotion that's made me a wreck washes away, quickly cleansed by fear. I turn slowly, my mouth parted but words refuse to come out.

I don't have the strength or courage to ask who's behind me.

But I don't have to.

I let out a breath as a bushy tail comes into view.

"Boots," I say, greeting the neighbor's tabby cat and add, "You scared me," with my hand over my heart.

She must've snuck in while the balcony door was open and I was busy mulling over my wretched married life. There's an archway between my house and the neighbor's, and Boots used to be a regular on this balcony. Taking a few steps inside the bedroom, I scoop up the small cat. Her fur is soft and she purrs with contentment the moment I pet her. I only have a moment, though. She gets fed up with attention quickly and I've been on the wrong end of her claws before.

"You know you're not supposed to be in here," I scold her. Suddenly feeling exhausted, my conviction wanes. I escort Boots back outside, setting her down and move to shut the door just as my phone rings behind me on the bed.

The balcony is at the end of the bedroom so I have to walk quickly to answer in time, but I do on the last ring.

"Hello?"

"Jules, how are you?" Kat's voice asks. "I was just calling to check in."

"A mess," I say and my throat is tight. Is this what a breakup feels like? Or is this what regret feels like? I'm not sure which is which anymore. I suppose the two are one and the same.

"God, I know ... it has to be rough." I nod my head but my lips are pressed into a thin line without any words wanting to come and contribute to the conversation.

"Do you want to talk about it?"

Closing my eyes, I shake my head even though I know she can't see; a moment later I'm able to tell her no.

"Hey, it's all going to be okay," Kat says as if it's a fact. "You know that, don't you?"

A small breath of disbelief leaves me. "No, Kat." I lay back on the bed and add, "No, I don't know it's going to be all right. It doesn't feel like it will."

"Stop it. Stop it right now." Although her tone is harsh, the pain behind her words is undeniable. "Not everything in life is good, but that doesn't mean you don't have a good life."

I lick my dry lips and close my eyes, lying back farther on the bed and trying to absorb my friend's advice.

"You have a great life, Jules. You really do."

"I thought I was okay. I thought I'd be able to move on. I thought I *was* moving on."

"You're going to, Jules."

My exhausted eyes stay shut tight, refusing to feel anymore and I hold my breath. "One day, probably sooner than you know it, it's going to feel normal without him. It's going to feel good without him. And there's not a single thing wrong with that."

"It doesn't feel like it's okay, though. It doesn't feel like it's all right to not be upset."

"It doesn't have to right now. You don't have to do

anything right now, except tell me you're going to come to my house tomorrow night."

A sniff is what she gets in response until I'm able to compose myself.

"Of course."

"Good, now … are you all right?"

I answer her honestly. "I'm not, but I think I will be."

"You *definitely* will be," she says with such conviction, I believe her. My body feels lighter as I scoot closer to the edge of the bed, ready to do something.

"Do you want to go out for dinner?" I ask Kat.

Kat takes a deep breath on the other end of the line and I know she's busy and can't. That's her *I wish I could* sigh. She's always busy with work. "I can't—"

"It's fine," I say, cutting her off. "I've got to get out of this house." I speak while looking up at the coffered ceilings in the bedroom. This house has too many memories in it.

"You go out and get some fresh air, maybe get some shopping in and I'll see you tomorrow night."

Nodding in agreement, I answer, "See you tomorrow."

"Love you, Jules." Kat's voice is soft when she tells me she loves me.

"I love you too." It's so true. I'd crumble into a complete mess without her.

As I rise from the bed, it groans slightly and I look back to find it in disarray. I take the time to pull the sheets tight and lay the comforter just right. I even fluff the pillows and place them where they're supposed to be.

As my feet pad against the old wooden floor, it creaks right where I know it should and that chill from earlier comes back to me. I look up at the balcony door and find it unlocked, which is odd. I swear I locked it.

Click. The sound is loud as I stare at the lock, my fingers still on the cold hard metal.

I never did like having a balcony in the bedroom. Jace told me it was a silly fear. I cross my arms, feeling unsteady and colder by the second. I tuck a strand of hair behind my ear, grabbing my phone and clutch then throw on a pair of faded blue jeans.

Unsteady is the feeling that's most recognizable. I'm not sure where I go from here. Worse, I don't know where I want to go.

All I know in this moment, with everything in me, is that I just want to get out of this house.

CHAPTER 26

MASON

Ticktock.

It's a bomb, not a clock.

Ticktock.

It's about time to go off.

Ticktock.

Prepare for the shock.

Ticktock.

It's the truth to unlock.

I stand facing the window in my father's office with my hands behind my back and don't bother turning around to greet him as the door opens. I watch as my cold gray eyes narrow in the reflection. The city traffic below is stirring with life, but it's silent up here. So many people surround us, but not one of them can save me. Not one of them would even give a fuck.

Julia would. *My sweetheart.* Or at least she would have days ago before she realized she needed to get away from me.

"Mason," my father says and I turn around, finally facing him and knowing I need to confront him along with everything else I've been running from. As much as I want to hold Jules close and pretend just being with her will make this right, I know it won't.

"Father," I say, greeting him with an icy tone in my voice, hating that I'm even related to this man. I stare into his eyes and see my own. Everything about him reminds me of what I'm becoming. I fucking hate it.

"We need to get over this," my father says and gestures between the two of us.

"We do." I clench my jaw, my pulse rushing faster. I rip my gaze away from his, staring down at my hands. "I don't think there should be any more ties." It pains me to tell him that. Even after all these years and everything he's done, I still feel a gaping hole in my chest at the thought of severing this relationship.

"Ties to what?" he asks.

"Between the two of us."

My father flinches as if I've struck him. But what did he expect?

"Watch your mouth," he says. I'm surprised he has the

nerve to admonish me as if what I'm saying is unspeakable.

"I want to walk away. I don't want to be tied to this anymore. I don't want to be associated with you."

"I'm your father, Mason. You can't walk away from that."

The fuck I can't. I bite down on my tongue to stop from blurting out that answer, gritting my teeth as he walks closer to the left side of the desk. I walk to the right, matching his pace, a careful dance of power that escalates the conversation.

"You need to just forgive—"

"I'll never forgive you for what you did to Avery," I say, looking my father in the eye as I say her name for the first time in months. Every muscle in me is wound tightly, waiting for his next move so I can destroy him and let out this rage.

His eyes flash with something—anger, maybe betrayal, I don't know what.

"I did what I had to do to protect you," he says, pushing out the words from between clenched teeth, but his nerve is shaken, unlike mine.

"She didn't deserve to be murdered." My hands ball into fists. Avery was a mistake. A fiery redhead with long legs and a smile that could kill. She had *mistake* written all over her.

I met her late one night at an event and I knew she was trouble. I knew it from the start but I needed a quick fuck. She tempted me and I took the bait. But I could never have imagined how it would all end.

"That's what happens when you blackmail a Thatcher."

My father practically spits. "She decided to roll the dice. She's the one who came to me with demands and tried to back us into a corner."

"You could have sent her to me." My muscles twitch with the need to pound my fist into his face as I take a step forward. "I would have told her the baby couldn't have been mine."

"If I'd known then—"

"You didn't have to know!" I shout, unable to control myself any longer. My throat feels raw as the words are ripped from me, screaming up my chest. "She wasn't innocent." I take a step toward my father and grab the edge of the desk to keep from gripping his collar and say, "But she didn't deserve to die."

"She did." My father's voice is hard, his back straight and his gaze full of confidence.

"She was pregnant!" I tell him. Hating how he could so easily dismiss her existence. He had her murdered. He didn't even think twice about ending her life.

"With a married man's child!" my father sneers, his face turning red as he leans in closer to me and I can't take it any longer.

I can't take the arrogance and justification of ending a person's life so easily. I clench my fist until my knuckles are white and punch my father in the jaw. His teeth crack from the weight of the blow. His head whips to the side as he falls to the floor, limp and shocked. My arm stings with the pain of impact.

It feels so fucking good to finally give him a piece of what he deserves.

He lays there for a moment, his hand over his mouth as a trickle of blood leaks from the corner of his lips. I shake out my hand, adrenaline rushing through my veins. I just barely restrain myself from kicking him in the ribs, from letting all this anger and pent-up guilt out on him.

"You ungrateful prick." He spits blood onto the floor and looks up at me with a menacing glare. "You chose some whore over your own family."

No, I'm choosing what's right. I'm choosing to be better than this life I was born into.

My father doesn't quit with his justification. "Anderson didn't want that kid. Think about what she would have done to him!"

The mention of Jace Anderson makes my gaze break from my father's. The memories come back and make my tense muscles spasm. I can't hear whatever my father's yelling at me. It's all white noise.

I may have been born a Thatcher and I'll die a Thatcher, but I refuse to be anything like my father. Not today, not ever.

"I won't forgive you." I force my body to relax. I've said what I came to say. This ends now. "I never will." I start to walk out, accompanied by the sound of my heart racing.

Just as my hand grips the doorknob, I finally get the balls to ask him.

One last thing to say. One final question.

Walking back to his desk with confident steps, I imagine his answer as if I already know it. He turns slightly from facing the window, still curled up on the floor behind his desk, looking at me as if he doesn't trust me. He shouldn't. Not with how I'm feeling at this moment.

I stop on the opposite side of the desk, my mind racing as I go back years and years. Back to only a boy who lost his mother. Scared, confused ... and angry.

"Mom didn't die from an overdose." The statement comes out accusatory and it's meant to. He wipes the blood from his mouth with the bright white sleeve of his dress shirt. He doesn't look me in the eye, doesn't acknowledge what I said in the least.

I take one step toward him, a large step that gets his attention. His gaze whips up to me. "Did you have her killed too?"

"How dare you!" His nostrils flare as he pins me with his gaze. "How dare you, you fucking ..." he trails off and doesn't finish. His shoulders are hunched forward as he grips his desk chair for balance to stand.

I'm struck by the powerful way he's affected. I've wondered for so long, months now. If he had Avery killed, maybe he did the same with my mother.

I flex my hand and swallow thickly, feeling the need to explain. My question was prompted by a gut feeling more than anything else. I don't remember much from around the time she died, but I remember how I felt. How the air between them was tense. How scared my mother was that he would find out her dirty little secret. "I know she was cheating—"

"Get out!" My father shouts at me, not holding anything back as he throws his chair to the side, putting all of his weight into it. It crashes against the bookshelf, several of the books tumbling to the floor as he slams his fists against his desk.

I turn my back on him, my fist pulsing in agony from the punch and my chest hurting with a pain I can't explain.

He pounds his fists again and again on the maple desk as I force myself to walk away from him.

Leaving my father alone in his office and promising myself never to see him again, never to speak to him, never to trust him. And never to be like him.

Never again.

CHAPTER 27

JULIA

I stare down at the neat piles of papers to my right in the dining room. My back is killing me and my shoulders are screaming in pain. It's so wrong that now that these contracts and files are sorted out, my first thought is to call Mason, to see if he's free and tell him that I miss him.

God, do I miss him.

He could ease my physical pains, but also that sick lonely feeling I have after going through three years of finances.

Three years of hard evidence of Jace cheating. Three long years compiled in black ink on white pages.

I glance at the email still open on my laptop. Mr. Walker will have more for me tomorrow. It makes my stomach lurch because I know I'll see more credit card statements for hotel charges during the day when he was supposed to be working, along with charges for jewelry and everything else he bought the women he kept on the side. I don't need to see it. That's the messed-up part of it all.

Selling the apartment and being done with it is the last of all the problems and loose ends Jace left.

I'll be fine financially; everything is going to be okay on that front. But I want to know how long it went on. I want to know at what point in my life I wasn't good enough for him anymore.

The wine in the glass is almost gone and it's late, but I pour myself another. We all have our vices and it turns out mine are cabernet and Mason Thatcher. My lips curl into a pathetic weak smile and then I take a sip of the sweet wine.

I stare at the open newspaper on the table. The one with a photograph of Mason and someone else. Someone *new*. It's not hard to admit that it hurts to see it, to think that he's moved on already. It hasn't even been two weeks since I saw him last. It has their picture but the accompanying article is about me being used by the playboy bachelor and left brokenhearted. They know nothing and I couldn't care less about what they think happened. What matters is that I am heartbroken.

Mason. I've stared at that photo for far too long praying it isn't true. Mostly because I'm selfish. I'm not ready to commit to him, or to anyone, but I want him all the same.

Sue has assured me it's all made up and the woman in the

photo is someone he dated long ago.

I take another gulp of wine and only look up from the same paragraph I've read five times when I hear my phone go off.

It's a text from Kat wanting my manuscript. Oh God.

It's a good thing I have an apartment up for sale, I suppose. Maybe I should thank my cheating deceased husband for that.

It takes a small sip before I have the courage to text her back, asking for an extension and then open my laptop to write. To let the words flow. If anything, I expect it to be about anger, grief, betrayal. But all that comes are thoughts of Mason's touch. How powerful his physical presence can be. How he can soothe my every pain. How he wants to do just that, and about how much I want it even more.

I let my head fall to the side when I remember him kissing me as he played my body right at this very spot that I'm sitting. My fingers never stop tapping on the keys as I relive the moment. I open my eyes and stare at the grain woven into the wooden table where I bent over for him. I confessed something so real, so painful and he made me feel alive and as though nothing else mattered.

I suck in a deep breath, hating that I left him the way that I did. I'm so damn broken. I don't understand why he wants me when it's obvious that I'm a wreck.

Biting down on my lip, I stare at the phone and think of texting him.

I miss you. I type in the words and then delete them.

I'm sorry. I stare at the two words that are so simple, yet mean so much.

I think I love you. That's what I should send him. Scare him away for good.

I delete the text as Kat messages me back. She's usually hard on me. Guilting me if I miss a deadline and reminding me about everyone else's schedules involved. It lights a fire under my bottom.

But all she's written this time is that it's okay and to take care of myself.

"Take care of myself," I whisper beneath my breath and let my fingers trail down the stem of the wineglass.

I wish Mason were here, but that's just an easy out.

This is supposed to hurt. It's supposed to be hard.

I want to crawl back to him and beg for forgiveness. Beg him to take away the pain again. It's selfish and I won't do that to him, but I'd be a liar if I said I didn't want to.

Chapter 28

Mason

"I just got an email." I hear Liam's irritation as the door opens. His light gray suit is sharp and crisp, but he looks like shit himself. His dirty blond hair is a mess on top of his head and the dark circles under his eyes prove he hasn't gotten much sleep.

"About what?" I ask. I don't let on that I already know what the email was about as I rest my elbows on the desk. Waiting for him to speak, I make a steeple with my pointer fingers. I know what this is about. My father's pulled the funds.

We're fucked. And I don't have a way out of this.

"What happened, Mason?" His question is drenched with desperation.

I swallow hard, hating that I owe Liam anything. I know I do. At the very least I owe him an explanation, but what can I tell him? My jaw clenches and I look down at my desk as I pick at my hands where a small cut mars my knuckles. I can't turn in my father. I don't have any hard evidence of his misdeeds but more than that, I can't bring myself to do it to my own father. That last part causes me more shame than I'm willing to admit.

I clear my throat and lean forward to face Liam.

"We have to back down or find new investors."

"Back down?" His wide eyes stare at me as though I'm the insane one here. Maybe I am. "We can't fucking back down. We've sunk millions into this!" I can practically see his heart racing out of his chest.

"I'm sorry, but—"

"What the fuck happened?" he shouts as he stands up, throwing the papers on the desk behind him. My blood heats as I glare at Liam.

"Sit down." The words come out harsh and as a demand. It gets his attention, like a child who's been scolded. I'll own up to failing him but I have my limits, and when it comes to business, I demand respect. He's still, almost frozen for a long moment and then he places both his hands flat on the desk and leans over, getting closer to my face. He's still a foot away, but it's too fucking close for my liking.

"Don't tell me what to do, Thatcher," he says low in his

throat. "This is going to ruin us. Ruin *me*," he hisses.

"We'll recover." I don't have the confidence my voice reflects. But I'll do whatever I have to in order to make this work. I have no intention of going anywhere. If I have to start from the bottom again and claw my way back up to the top, so be it.

"You need to get over whatever it is that's going on between you and your father. Whatever the fuck it is, just let it go."

He glares at me long and hard. Waiting for me to comply, but it's not going to happen. I may not be sending my father away to prison for life, but I'm through with him for good. I'm sure as fuck not going to take his money.

"I have a few meetings tomorrow with Marcus Jennings and Austin Hook." I lean back in my seat, daring him to come closer. His body tenses as he turns his head in disbelief, still leaning over my desk.

He shakes his head, looking bewildered. "How could you do this to me?" He barely gets out the words. He pushes off the desk, shaking his head again and walking a few feet away before looking back at me.

I can see each emotion as they flow through him and finally he settles on anger. "Is it because of Anderson?" he asks and my heart stops in my chest.

I stand up straight out of instinct. Out of the need to figure out how much he knows.

"What the fuck does he have to do with this?" My voice is deathly low as my eyes narrow; my muscles are coiled and ready for a fight. *What does he know?*

He gives me a confused look in return. "'He?'" Liam tilts his head and it's then that I realize he was talking about Jules and using her married name. My heart sinks lower and a cold sweat breaks out over my body. *Fuck!*

"I'm talking about the bitch you've been fucking." My body turns to stone, stuck in place by an anger I can't control. Everything goes red as he keeps talking, oblivious to my reaction. "Everything's changed since she's come around."

I crack my neck to the side, deciding to ignore it. To give him one chance. That's all he'll get. "It has nothing to do with her."

"Oh yeah? She didn't convince you not to make amends with your father? Or fuck him over or fuck me over?" With each question, his voice gets louder and louder.

"She doesn't know shit about my father and she has no place here or in any of this."

He flashes me a cocky grin. "Really gets you worked up, doesn't it?" He rounds the desk as he talks. "Is it because she dumped your ass on Madison Avenue?" The question comes with a laugh and he closes the space between us. I already know this is going to end badly; I'm only waiting for the right moment to strike at this point. "What'd you do that had her running out of that car, Mason? You fuck her over too? Just like you fucked—"

I can't stop what's started. He shouldn't have brought up Jules. I can't control myself when it comes to her.

My fist comes out of nowhere, hitting him square on the jaw and sending him flying backward. Twice in one week I've hit a man. And for the second time, I don't give a shit.

My knuckle flares where the cut from the last punch is still healing and my shoulder screams with pain from the impact. My vision clouds, anger making it redder by the second. Everything rages inside. The anger of her leaving me, the disappointment of my father, the regret of what I've done all mix into a deadly concoction. I take two steps forward with my hands up, ready to beat the piss out of him, ready for the fight he obviously wants, but he's limp on the floor, blood leaking from his nose.

Crouching down, I grip the lapels of his jacket, pulling harder than I should but I can't stop myself, panic warring against everything else. He's motionless and unresponsive. I fist his jacket in my hands, shaking him. "Liam!" Dread courses through me. What the hell did I do? I slap him lightly across the face, but he doesn't respond.

I hold a hand over his nose just to make sure he's breathing. The warm air confirms that he is. *Thank fuck.* My body aches as I stand, running my hands through my hair and then down my face as I pace the floor.

I look up to the clock and I only have five, maybe ten

minutes before everyone arrives at the office. I lean my forearm against the wall of windows, feeling defeated and like a fucking idiot. This isn't who I am now. This isn't the man I wanted to be. I lean all of my weight into the glass. I'm spiraling, all from the mention of her name.

The realization that I just knocked out Liam weighs heavily on my shoulders. The one man I could occasionally refer to as a friend.

I stare at my own reflection as I realize how badly I've fucked up.

It doesn't take long before I decide I need to call an ambulance and I'm very much aware they'll call the police. I clench my jaw and swallow my pride. *It'll be a fucking spectacle.*

He shouldn't have talked about Jules, though.

He had to know this was going to happen.

CHAPTER 29

JULIA

Why do you haunt me so?
You take control of my thoughts,
You consume my sleep.
How do you wound me still?
You need to leave me alone,
I'm not yours to keep.

"It can't be true." I only parted my lips, but the words tumbled out without thinking. Sitting around the same small table in the coffee shop feels surreal as I read the article. We were just here not even a month ago and it's unreal how everything has changed.

"You broke him," Maddie says somewhat jokingly to try to lighten the mood.

His company, his friendships, his father. I know the tabloids make up a good portion of their content, but the mug shot is something that can't be denied.

"It's all dropped and he'll be fine," Sue says airily as if it's no big deal.

The newspaper falls to the table and the faint sound of the paper rustling is all I can hear.

"I don't understand what happened," I say, thinking out loud. "He never said anything to me about his father or about the business."

Sue shrugs. "Sometimes people don't talk about the things that bother them. He'll be fine." How can I not know, though? I shared so much of myself with Mason. I was raw and open and giving of so much of me. I know he did the same. I could feel it between us. It wasn't one sided. I hid the darkest secrets from him ... and he did the same with me. A new form of regret wraps itself around my throat. *I should make sure he's all right like he did for me.* That's an excuse I can use to run back to him.

"Coffee?" Kat asks as she sits down and places a hot ceramic mug in front of me. It's been mixed with an almost offensive amount of creamer and the color matches my cream accent pillows at home... just the way I like it.

With a grateful smile, I accept it and blow over the top, inhaling the smell and trying to feel normal. Or as normal as I can, all things considered. Kat's busy reading over the manuscript on her phone, but whether or not it will do is nowhere on my mind. All I can think about is the fact that Mason was there for me, so many times. He needs someone right now. The only question is whether or not he'd let me in.

She murmurs the lines as she opens the book.

> Sweet lies you told me, beautiful forever.
> A dream or a terror, I craved it, whichever.
> A taste so sweet, too much to say no,
> I couldn't resist and you couldn't let go.
> Your healing touch and comforting kiss—
> But I never thought it would end like this.

Kat tilts her head, her lips stopping mid-poem and she gives me a questioning look as she says, "Is this one about Jace?"

The book was supposed to be about mourning and loss. It is, but it's a deceptive cocktail of the two men. I loved and lost both of them.

All I can do is take a sip of coffee and try not to choke on the lie as I say, "I don't remember."

"So have you heard from him?" Maddie asks me, thankfully saving me from Kat's interrogation.

My ponytail swishes along the crook of my neck as I shake my head no. He got the message that we were over after I repeatedly refused his calls. I don't think he'll ever reach out to me again.

"Have you called him?" Maddie asks.

"Not yet," I tell her. "Or, no. No, I haven't." *Thump, thump, thump,* my poor little heart won't stay where it's supposed to and I hide in my coffee cup again.

Her voice is hopeful as she scoots forward, the sound of the stool scratching against the floor making an annoying screech. "You should."

"I don't know ... I want to. He was ..." I trail off as I run my fingers up and down the cup and stare at a lone muffin in front of me. I haven't eaten since I heard about Mason this morning.

"I think you should," Maddie says softly.

"I think you should shut your mouth and let things happen as they should," Sue bites out and Maddie merely gives her a look of defiance.

"She breaks up with him and he falls apart—" Maddie looks like she's about to go off on Sue, but she doesn't get much out.

"Stop it," Sue says. "That's not her fault." Sue points at the paper and adds, "This has nothing to do with Jules."

"You don't know that." Maddie's response is soft as she looks down to her own blueberry muffin and picks at the top of it. "Everyone's saying he's heartbroken."

"Jesus, Maddie!" Sue snaps. "Jules, this is not your fault and you don't owe him anything. Don't go back to a man because of guilt." Her voice cracks and her eyes hold a warning. "Please. If you want to reach out to him, do it for any other reason than feeling guilty or like you owe him." There's a tear at my chest, an open wound knowing Sue is speaking from experience.

"I wasn't trying to hurt him, Maddie." I can't respond to Sue right now, my throat feels tight. "I didn't think he'd care, to be honest ..." I don't know if that's true. I wasn't thinking of him when I ended it. I was only thinking of me. Of my anger. "It just happened so fast and it was too much."

"There's nothing wrong with fast," Kat says, surprising the three of us. It's then that I notice she hasn't moved past the first page. "Evan and I got engaged in three months."

Their story was a whirlwind romance. Everyone's story is different. Maybe this is regret or guilt pushing me toward Mason, but it's different from what Sue went through. I swear our story has to be different.

My heart begs me to stop, but I have to ask them a question that's kept me up the last three nights I've dreamed of Mason. It's killing me slowly and carefully, destroying everything I thought I knew. "Isn't it wrong to fall for someone *else* so quickly after Jace?"

"No," Kat says and shakes her head. "It's wrong to throw something away because you're afraid of it, though." Her voice is full of regret, but it didn't stop her from telling me exactly what she thinks.

"You guys are giving me whiplash." I swallow thickly and brush the loose locks out of my face, resting my elbows on the table and burying my face in my hands. "I shouldn't be with him, I should be with him. I hurt him by breaking up with him, but I shouldn't be with him if I feel regret. I don't know what to think!" I say, my voice raw and the words tearing their way up my throat.

"What do you want, Jules?" Sue asks me, not missing a beat although my other two friends only stare at me with questions and guilt of their own. "Love isn't about thinking, it's only about what you feel." Of all the women in this group, I'm not sure I should take her advice on love, but she says it with such conviction that I believe it. And I trust her.

"I feel like I've been sad for too long," I say. "I feel like I deserve to be punished for moving on. I feel like I miss Mason. Like really miss him. And I know I hurt him." I brush my fingers under my eyes and suck in a breath to keep myself from falling to pieces. "I didn't know it would be like this. I feel like life was spinning out of control and he was the one steady thing and I was taking advantage of that." My fingers tremble as I press my palms against my eyes, finally finishing my thoughts. "I don't know if I'm running away from all this hurt or running to him." I swallow and whisper, "Maybe some of both? And it scares me."

It's too much to take in and process, but I need all this mayhem to stop.

"You don't have to know. You don't have to do anything," Kat says. Her phone's flipped over on the table and as soon as I notice that, I also notice all three women staring at me with sympathy. Waiting for me. I don't deserve this. I don't know how I ended up so close with these women but without them, I'd be so lost.

"You can take as much time as you need," Maddie says with a small nod.

That's the problem, though. I wanted things to be slow, but he was a force I couldn't control. My body bowed down to his and I would have been swallowed whole if I gave any more of myself to him.

It doesn't stop me from wanting him and the way I feel when I'm with him. He was right that first night when he said he'd make me forget everything but his name and what he'd done to me.

"Are you sure it's not wrong? Because it feels like the worst kind of wrong." I glance at each of the girls, feeling like whatever they tell me will propel me in the direction I need to go.

"It's scary," Maddie says, shifting in her seat and breaking eye contact.

"Love is terrifying," Kat adds.

"It's not wrong. You haven't done anything wrong and you should do what you want to do. Even if that's breaking every bachelor's heart in New York City." A soft, playful smile greets me as I look at Sue. She nudges me and reaches for the paper. "This wasn't your fault, but I can't say I'm not curious about the gossip ... and that I don't think there was something good about you two being together."

CHAPTER 30

MASON

Anger management. The paper crinkles in my hand as I crumple it.

No charges were pressed, but I'm sure Liam's getting a kick out of the anger management classes the judge ordered me to attend. *Prick.* I know the asshole would have pushed the issue further if it wasn't for the company. He wants to save face and hold this over me so I can do his bidding.

That's not going to fucking happen. I'll take on all the debt if I have to and do it myself. The project is canceled; I'm taking the hit and dissolving the company. It's better that I'm alone. It's as simple as that.

I drop the empty bottle of whisky in the trash can as well

as the notice regarding the anger management course. The glass bottle clinks against the metal frame of the photograph. I stare down into the bin, the shattered glass marring the photo of the picture-perfect family. It's destroyed ... but really, it's always been that way.

I'm tired and angry, and tired of being angry too. This isn't what I wanted or planned. I wanted more. For me, that meant Jules. With my fingers pinching the bridge of my nose, I lean back against the kitchen wall.

Call it what you want. Out of everything in life, she's the only thing I know I truly want. That should mean something.

I make my way upstairs, walking slowly and dreading another night alone in this empty house. It never bothered me much before, but I can't fucking stand the silence now.

Someone knocks three times at the front door and I still with my hand on the banister.

I wait a moment, wondering who the fuck would be here this late at night, even though only one name comes to mind. I steel myself for the worst, thinking it's my father. I can't face him right now. Not after what he's done and what I accused him of. It's only after another three knocks that I force myself to face the consequences. I open the door with a swift pull, prepared to turn him away, but my voice is caught in my throat.

Jules's baby blue eyes look at me with a mix of emotions. Fear, sorrow ... hope. The chill of the wind spreads goosebumps along her arms and blows her long brunette hair off her shoulders. She looks to her left and then right, pulling her leather jacket tighter around her and taking a small step toward me.

"Mason," she says and licks her lush lips, painted with that same color I've grown to expect from her. "I—" She stops to clear her throat and looks away again as I stand numb in the doorway.

Fate's delivered her to me. I can't let her go this time. I won't.

"I was hoping we could talk?" Her voice is timid and her heels click on the cement porch as she shifts in place. Her tight blue jeans hug her curves, although the loose cream blouse beneath her jacket leaves much to the imagination. I know what's under there, though.

I don't say a word, too afraid of scaring her off. Instead I take a step to the side and open the door wider, waiting for her to walk in.

Her cheeks and the tip of her nose are a beautiful rosy red from the bite of the night air.

She hesitantly steps inside and looks around as if she hasn't been here enough times to have the place memorized. I close the door and stare at the lock a moment too long before turning it.

"Mason, I'm sorry." Jules's voice calls to me as I turn around to face her. I watch her swallow and then bite down on her bottom lip. She's worried and apologetic, but I don't give a fuck about the past. I never did. I care about what she wants now.

"Why are you here, Jules?" I ask her in a deep voice. It's rougher than I intended, but it's all I can manage.

"I heard about what happened," she says. She fidgets as she waits for my response, but I don't give her one. I'm not interested in talking about anything but us. I don't want to taint her with the bullshit. "I just wanted to say I'm sorry for hurting you," she says in a tight voice full of agony.

"Is that all?" I say and it takes all the air I have in my lungs. Taking a step forward and closing the space between us, my heart thumps chaotically in my chest.

She twists her fingers around one another nervously. "I also," she starts to say and then swallows. "I was wondering if you still ... if you were interested ..."

"In what?" My eagerness gets the best of me. *Make this easy for me, Jules, and I'll make everything right. I promise you, sweetheart, I'll make it up to you.*

"If you'd like to maybe go out again? If that's what we were doing?" A nervous huff of a laugh accompanies her proposition. I stare at her a moment, thinking it's just too good to be true. She came back to me. There's a saying about that, but it's not meant for real life. It's not meant for men like me.

"If you still want me," Jules adds, the raw vulnerability so thick in her voice.

"I never stopped wanting you," I say, my voice barely a murmur. Her doe eyes never leave mine as I gently push her jacket off her shoulders. If she thinks I don't want her, she'll know better soon enough.

"Mason," she says and gasps as I lean down and kiss her neck. Maybe it's the alcohol or maybe it's just that my body knows hers. But I'm not waiting for apologies or excuses or explanations.

I need to *feel* her.

"Mason, stop." She pushes her hands against my chest, shrugging her jacket back on as I take a step back. "I need you to know that I'm worried we're going too fast. I'm worried that this isn't going to last."

A deep breath steadies me as I stare down at my sweetheart. "I told you, Jules. If you're with me, then you're with me and that's all there is to it." I take her hand in mine and kiss one knuckle, then another.

"Mason," she whimpers as if I've broken her heart. She has no idea. I turn her hand over and kiss her pulse, my heart beating faster.

"No more of this running from me or from us, Jules. Are you with me?" I ask her, feeling more vulnerable than I ever have in my entire life. I whisper, "Are you mine?"

"I don't know that my heart is mine to give, Mason. It's broken and I don't know if it will heal the right way." Jules sniffs and looks ashamed, but she has no idea how much I understand. I truly do.

Grief is a journey and she doesn't have to go it all alone.

I wrap my arm around her waist and pull her into me.

"You don't have to be perfect, Jules, in order to be perfect for me." I kiss her hair and hope that she can understand. "I want you how you are today, and tomorrow I'll want you how you are then."

Jules buries her head into my chest, her hair brushing against my chin and I kiss the top of her head. "Why are you so perfect, Mason?" she says and relaxes in my embrace. "How do you know just the right words to say?" Her voice is soft and relaxed as she molds her body to mine and that's when I know I've won her over.

"I'm not perfect, Jules." My heart aches in my chest, knowing just how imperfect I am. And how imperfect I am *for her*. She has no idea. We aren't meant to fit together, but I'll force the pieces to line up and pretend it's meant to be.

For her. Because I owe her that much.

"I can't tell you how happy I am that you came back," I whisper and run my hand in soothing circles along her back.

CHAPTER 31

JULIA

I asked you to leave.
I need to be alone.
But you stayed in my head.
My heart and my home.
I asked you to leave me,
But you won't go away.
When I go to find you tomorrow,
I only hope that you'll stay.

Mason's bedroom is so much darker than mine. Full of deep grays and dark wood. It matches the rest of his home, I suppose. His curtains are thick velvet and shut tight. Even with hardly any light, I can see him, all of him. His muscles ripple in the faint light. It makes Mason seem so much more dominating, which is criminal.

He already owns me, consuming me with his presence. But right now, at this very moment as he towers over me, skimming his fingers over my sensitized skin, I'm weaker for him than I've ever been in my entire life.

"Mason." I murmur his name as he lays me down on his bed. I turn my head to the side and arch my back as he leaves open-mouth kisses down my neck. We're both naked, but it's more than that. So much more. We've been here before plenty of times, but this is different. We're bared to each other.

"If we do this, can you promise me one thing?" My heart is pounding in my chest as I lay back on the bed, because I feel like this is the end. It's putting so much to rest and moving on toward the unknown. I'm terrified that I'll fall and he'll let me shatter when he's done with me.

"What?" He whispers the question between kisses.

"Please don't hurt me," I beg him. "I want you and I want what we have ..." I trail off, barely able to breathe. "But promise if you want me to go, you'll do it easy and as soon as you know." He braces his forearms on either side of my head and looks down at me with an intense look in his gray eyes that pierces my lungs, stopping me from breathing.

"You need to stop this." His voice is hard, but it always is when I say something he doesn't like. "Do you understand?"

I nod my head and say, "Yes." I really do. I want this to stop and for *us* to begin.

"Don't hide from me, Jules. Don't run from me," Mason tells me with an authority that can't be denied.

I nod my head in complete agreement. I'm tired of running and denying myself what I really want. "No more secrets," I say into the hot air between us.

Mason pulls away, looking at me as if he's going to tell me something. The silence and tension grow, but no words come. Instead he crashes his lips to mine and pushes his body against me, forcing me to spread my legs for him.

And I do, I let him have all of me.

His fingers trail down between my legs as my core heats. He doesn't stop nipping and kissing all over my heated body, his hands roaming freely, taking in every inch of me. I'm helpless beneath him. Falling deeper and deeper into the darkness and loving how overwhelming it all is.

I missed this. God, how I missed this.

He groans in the crook of my neck, a sexy deep sound that makes my body arch toward him as if drawn even closer to him by an undeniable pull. His heated skin brushes against mine as he pushes himself inside of me.

My mouth opens and I stare up at him, his steel gray eyes holding my gaze as he enters me, slowly stretching me and not stopping until he's fully inside of me.

My heart beats faster, my body numb and on edge, waiting for him to move and take me how he wants me. Rough, raw, and making me his.

His fingers dig into my hips, pinning me down as he pulls out slightly and then slams back in, forcing a whimper from me. My body bucks instinctively, but I never break eye contact. I can't. He holds me captive beneath his gaze.

He does it over and over again until I'm so wet and hot for him that he easily slips in and out, each time forcefully smacking against my clit.

My body writhes and begs me to move away; it's too much, too intense. But that's just how Mason is. I knew it when I met him. More than that, I need him. I need this.

I love you, my heart whispers but I don't say it aloud. Small whimpers of pleasure spill from my lips with each thrust and I swear I'm close to admitting it. So close.

He groans low in his throat as he speeds up his relentless thrusts, resting his forehead against mine and kissing me mercilessly. Our lips barely touch, but they do, kiss after kiss after kiss. A series of slow kisses with our hearts racing fast beg me to confess.

He steals the breath from my lungs. His hot body makes mine burn with desire. I cling to him, wrapping my legs around him and digging my nails into his shoulder.

Higher and higher he pushes me.

The pleasure comes in small waves, dim at first but growing stronger and stronger. They threaten to overwhelm me as my fingers and toes tingle. The crash will shatter me, I know it. I don't beg him to stop. I don't try to pull away. I want it, I crave it, I'm desperate for him to ruin me.

"Mason!" I cry out as the wave consumes me, pulling me under in an intense orgasm that paralyzes my body. It's Mason's cue to devour me and he does, fucking me with no regard for the state I'm in. He's chasing his own release, pounding into me recklessly and extending my pleasure that much longer.

I scream out as he whispers, "Mine," in the crook of my neck again and again. His throaty voice gets louder as he fucks me harder. I can't do a damn thing but take everything he's giving me. And I do, with my nails digging into his skin and his masculine scent surrounding me. His large body suffocating me in the most delicious way.

It's only when he stills deep inside of me as I pant under him, desperately trying to breathe, that I'm able to moan out my pleasure. His thick cock pulses and the wetness between my thighs leaks between us.

He doesn't stop holding me.

He doesn't stop kissing me.

I almost don't tell him. I almost hide from him, but I promised him I wouldn't.

"I love you," I whisper and give that piece of me to him too. He doesn't say it back, but I know he heard it.

He kisses me without mercy, soothing my pain and taking everything I have.

CHAPTER 32

MASON

H*ow long is long enough?* I keep thinking it with every second that passes. As if I'm not a complete fraud for asking Jules to marry me.

It's been two weeks of things falling perfectly into place. She's still waiting for the other shoe to drop. For this fantasy we're living in together to crumble into pieces. I won't let it, though. I'll give her everything she wants and that includes a ring, a sense of security that will seal us together and truly put our respective pasts behind us.

Financially, with my business in shambles and the money tied up in contracts I'm obligated to fulfill but can't, I'm fucked. I was smart enough to incorporate the business as an LLC, though. Personally, all I have is my house and stocks. It's nothing compared to her bank account. But I'm stable and when the contracts are finalized and the business assets are split, I'll be able to give her even more. I'm surprised she hasn't asked, but I'm prepared if that's a concern for her.

My eyes focus on the deep red petals scattered on every surface. I want her. I don't care about anything else anymore.

The only thing I give a damn about is making Jules mine in every way.

I don't want her to tell me no. I can't stand the thought of her turning me down or worse, if simply asking her to be my wife could push her away.

It doesn't matter how fast she is if she runs though, how quickly she'll turn me down and try to hide. I'll find her, I'll catch her and I'll wait for her. Always.

I close the small black velvet box, making the vision of the four-carat, cushion-cut diamond vanish and shove it into my pocket. Letting a heavy breath leave me, I turn and look at the living room. It's obvious. So damn obvious that I'm going to propose.

The second she walks in here and sees the crystal vases of deep red roses on every surface, she's going to know what I have planned.

I can see her now, standing in the doorway, gripping onto the frame while her beautiful blue eyes go wide and she breathes in the floral scent. The lights are low and the tea lights are scattered.

I'm not a romantic man by nature, but for her and for this ... Hopefully for the start of our lives together, I can do romance. *All for her.* I'll pretend to be someone else until both of us believe it.

At the sound of the doorknob turning, my heart skips in my chest, hammering harder than I anticipated. I take a step back, pulling the box from my pocket and preparing to get down on my knee. My blood heats and anxiety suddenly washes through me. It's really happening. I'm really going to ask her to marry me. The thought itself calms me.

Of course I am. *I love her.*

I run my hand through my hair as she steps forward enough to come through the doors. I thought she'd be astonished by the sight of the room. I imagined her taking it all in, but she's only looking at me.

"Julianna Lynn Summers, I would be honored—" I start and already I've fucked up. I had this damn thing rehearsed. I thought I had it all memorized but having to look up at her, and not knowing what she's going to say ... I stumbled over my words.

Jules covers her mouth with a gasp, letting the front door shut slowly behind her. Her shoulders hunch forward some as her purse falls to the ground. I knew she'd be emotional; I just wish the shock would wane so I could see which side of her was winning out. The side that loves me and wants to live in the moment, or the side stuck in the past and afraid to move on.

Jules takes a few steps forward when I don't continue, her thin heels clicking on the polished wood floors as she places her hands on my shoulders and starts to lower herself to the ground, but that's not how I want her. I don't know how I'm able to wrap an arm around her long legs and look up at her, still holding the ring out although she's staring into my eyes. Her skin is soft beneath my touch.

"Jules, I love you and I want to spend every day of my life with you." I hesitate to say the words but I have to, even if she says she can't. "I want you as my wife," I tell her and watch her facial expression crumple with a hint of pain reflected in her eyes as I say the words.

"I love you too, Mason." She barely gets out the words as she covers her face with both her hands and then wipes under her eyes. Her eyes are glossy with tears and her voice is choked as she says it again. "I love you and I didn't know if I could ..." Hearing her start her confession breaks my heart and I rise just enough to hold her. She wraps her arms around my shoulders, gripping onto me as though she needs me to stand. And in so many ways, she does. She needs someone there and I'll always be that person for her.

So long as she'll let me.

She pulls away slightly, trying to pull herself together as she brushes her hair out of her face and looks away, taking a calming breath.

"I want all of you, Jules," I tell her as I cup her chin in my hand and force her to look at me. "When you're upset, I want to know so I can make you smile. When you're angry, just tell me. I'll let you take it out on me however you need, then make you come so hard you'll forget you ever felt anything other than bliss. I want the real you. Always. I never want you to hide from me."

Those lush lips part and a soft breath escapes her as she stares into my eyes. She's searching for something. She better not fucking wonder if everything I've just said is true or not.

"I want the same from you, Mason." I'm surprised at her response. I stay still on the ground, wondering how she could think for a second I wouldn't share all of me with her. Not my past, though. She doesn't know shit about that and she never will. None of it. I'm going to fix it all and keep it hidden in the shadows and buried nine feet deep where it all belongs.

She kneels on the floor in front of me and takes my jaw in both her hands, planting a soft sweet kiss on my lips. Her touch calms all my worries. It dispels the demons threatening to surface. She does this to me. She makes me a better person and I desperately want to be that man for her.

She speaks with her eyes closed, her lips close to mine and her hot breath filling the air between us. Her long, thick lashes are damp with her tears as she tells me, "I love you for you. The good and the bad. And I do want to be with you, Mason." Her voice is pained and I can't help but reach out and hold her, pulling her closer to me. "I need you," she whispers.

I kiss the crook of her neck. "All I need is your love."

"You have it, Mason."

She has yet to answer; I need to hear her tell me yes. I want to be good enough to be her husband and if I'm not today, then tomorrow I'll be better. I'm determined and she needs to know that. I put my hands on her shoulders.

"I love you, Jules. Will you marry me?" I ask her, looking deep into her eyes.

She gives me a sweet smile, almost a shy one as she sniffles and finally gives me everything I need by saying, "I love you too. Yes." Her words come out as if it's obvious. As if it's only natural.

I finally breathe a deep sigh of relief, heaving in the air and holding her close to me. I stand up, still carrying her and swing her in my arms as I rise.

I kiss up her neck and every inch of her exposed skin, making her let out a small, feminine laugh and push away from me slightly. This is the only kind of pushing I ever want her to do again. From this day forward, she's mine.

I only set her down so I can take out the ring from the box. I watch as Jules's eyes widen once again. "Oh my gosh," she says softly, eyeing the ring as though it's the most beautiful thing she's ever seen.

"Do you like it?" I ask her as I slip the box into my pocket and hold the ring out for her.

She bites her bottom lip as she nods vigorously and says,

"Mason, it's beautiful." Finally, she looks up at me as I slip the ring onto her finger. "I love it," she whispers.

A small breath leaves her as she rubs her fingers over my five o'clock shadow and gently kisses me. I've never felt anything like what I feel for her. Seeing my ring on her finger makes it seem as though it's all going to be all right.

As long as the past will stay buried where it belongs.

CHAPTER 33

JULIA

Lies lies go away,
The sins are all from yesterday.
We tried to run, you tried to beat us.
Now we're ruined, left defeated.

The frame clicks into place and I turn it over in my hands and smile. I straighten my back and hold up the heavy silver frame. This isn't for hanging out here where everyone can see. It's silly really, but I wanted it framed.

My engagement ring clinks against the silver frame as I hold it up, the sunlight from the large bay window in Mason's house, well our house now, reflecting off the glass as I read the words.

A New Love and New Beginning.

It's a picture of us from the first article about us that was run in the papers. Back when I didn't know how to feel about the two of us. When I was riddled with guilt and pain and not seeing things clearly, I hated that we were in the papers at all. But I loved the candid photo.

I happened to come across it online the other day and when I read it, I lost it. Mason had to come in and find out why I was crying. He's always worried that I'm going to break down. I wish he wasn't so concerned for me. Yes, I'm emotional, but I know what I want. *I want him.* Something as simple as this article shouldn't get me so emotional, especially since half the facts aren't even true. But I love that our story has a beginning that was captured. I love that everyone around us knew.

I would never have thought that this article would give me a sense of pride and bring back a memory I want to be reminded of. A night when two lost souls knew they needed each other, even if we were too blind or stubborn to see it, we felt it.

"Finally," I say. It's framed and perfect. Just how I wanted it.

I hear Mason's rough chuckle as he walks into the kitchen and wraps his hands around my hips then plants a kiss on my shoulder.

I have to close my eyes as he hums and places his hand on my lower belly. He wants a baby. The very thought warms my heart and makes my head fall back against his broad chest. Wedding first, though. I want it all with him.

"Soon," I say softly with my eyes closed.

"What's this?" Mason asks, picking up the frame and reading the article left on the counter from where I cut out the photo. I watch his eyebrows raise as he reads the first few lines and he looks at me questioningly.

"I was going to put it on *my* nightstand," I tell him softly, waiting for his reaction. I'm still adjusting to moving in. I'll never sell my family home but I'm happier here, away from all the reminders of what used to be.

With no response, he sets the frame down and kisses me again. It's soft and sweet, but it lasts. My heart swells each time he kisses me like this. When he pulls away, he grins at me. It's a cocky one that lets me know he thinks he's got me all tied up in knots. And he does.

"Why this one?" he asks me.

Truthfully, I'm not sure I can vocalize why I want this particular one on my nightstand, so I just shrug.

"I just want it," I tell him simply and my easy response makes him smile.

"Well if you want it, then it's all yours."

That right there is why it was so easy to fall for this man. It's simple and natural. No rhyme or reason. It just feels right.

I set the frame down on the counter. It's not at all a lazy weekend; I have to write like crazy to get this manuscript in before the deadline, but I'm doing everything I can to procrastinate.

"You want a drink?" Mason offers, his voice dripping with sex appeal. He has a sexy grin on his lips and I know he wants to stay in and do bad things tonight.

I can't resist him, so I nod my head and his smile widens, filling me with warmth. I'll never get enough of him and how he makes me feel.

I pick up the envelope on top of the pile of mail sitting to my right as he heads to the fridge. The envelope tears easily and a handwritten letter slips out.

I feel my forehead crease as I unfold the thick cream parchment. Who sends a letter like this in a plain envelope? Before I read it, I check the envelope again. My name is there, but there's no return address.

Dear Julia,

It pains me to tell you this, but I can't stand to watch from a distance as you fall into a trap. Your husband was murdered. I know this is going to shock you, but I have proof. You may not believe me but I pray that you do.

Mason Thatcher murdered him. Don't trust him. Don't let him know that you know. If he finds out, you won't be safe.

My blood runs cold as I stand at the counter, my heart racing out of my chest. There's more written, but I can't read it. A shiver rolls through my body and everything seems to blur.

There's no way this is true. There's no way, yet my fingers tremble and my gaze shifts from the letter to the man accused, standing only feet from me.

My eyes dart from Mason's back as he rummages in the fridge, then back to the paper.

My heart thumps.

Murdered. Jace wasn't murdered. I deny it all, swallowing thickly.

I reread the letter, blinking and taking it in. My lips move with the words, but I can't breathe. I can't focus.

The handwritten letters seem to swirl together into a cloud of distrust. My vision fades and I feel so fucking dizzy. I back up slowly, pushing from the island and letting the feet of the stool scrape against the tile. Mason looks up at the noise and my weak legs barely hold me up as I grip the stool, the paper crinkling in my hand, my bare feet padding against the cold floor.

My head shakes on its own. That's not true. It's not true. It can't be true.

"Jules?" Mason's voice is riddled with concern and something else. Something I never registered before, but I can hear it now. I can see it on his face as I barely breathe and look up at him.

"The—" I can't bring myself to confess what I've just read. It's a lie. It has to be a lie. What a cruel lie it is. But Mason's response is throwing me off.

He's careful as he sets a bottle of beer on the counter, squaring his shoulders, all humor gone from his face and something else, *someone* else, stands in his place.

"Mason?" I barely get out his name.

"What is it?" he asks me in a voice so menacing, fear lights a fire deep in the marrow of my bones. No. I shake my head. "Mason, no," I say as my throat goes dry and my words crack. *He didn't do anything. He didn't even know Jace.*

This isn't real. My fist grips the stool tighter and I struggle to react. This is a nightmare. It has to be.

I'm caught between my need to run to somewhere I can think and the need to know the truth. I need the truth. No more lies; no more secrets.

He promised.

He loves me.

There's just no way.

"Did you do it?" The question leaves me in a single weak breath and in an instant, something snaps into place. As if he's very aware of what I'm saying. As if he's been waiting for this.

No. My body turns to ice; my blood and lungs freeze and I can't believe this is reality. It can't be true.

Mason takes a step forward, around the island and it breaks me from my denial.

It's my cue to run, a natural instinct that takes over. The stool falls hard, crashing to the tiled floor as I take off, but Mason's faster, gripping my waist and making me jerk backward. I cry out from fear and he releases me, only for me to fall onto the floor. His large frame towers over me, his hands up as if he's approaching a wild animal. I feel as if I am just that. My eyes wide, my heart pounds in my chest. *Thump, thump, thump.*

"Did I do what?" he asks, his eyes narrowed and with a coldness I haven't seen before. This isn't the man I know.

My bottom lip wobbles, the small bit of strength vanishing as I take in the raw truth. "Did you kill my husband?"

About the Author

Thank you so much for reading my romances. I'm just a stay at home Mom and an avid reader turned Author and I couldn't be happier.

I hope you love my books as much as I do!

More by Willow Winters
www.willowwinterswrites.com/books

Made in United States
Troutdale, OR
12/11/2023